MacGregor's Book
Nook Discard
202 North Main Street
Yreka, CA 96097
(530) 841-2664

**Also available from Piper J. Drake
and Carina Press**

Hidden Impact
Deadly Testimony

Also available from Piper J. Drake

Extreme Honor
Ultimate Courage
Absolute Trust

PIPER J. DRAKE

CONTRACTED DEFENSE

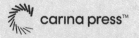

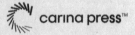 carina press™

ISBN-13: 978-1-335-89567-7

Recycling programs
for this product may
not exist in your area.

Contracted Defense

Copyright © 2018 by Piper J. Drake

This edition published by arrangement with Harlequin Books S.A.

® and TM are trademarks of the publisher. Trademarks indicated with
® are registered in the United States Patent and Trademark Office, the
Canadian Intellectual Property Office and in other countries.

www.CarinaPress.com

Printed in U.S.A.

To Corbin. Thank you for coming into my life just when my heart needed your love.

CONTRACTED
DEFENSE

Chapter One

"The Dalmore, neat, with a water back and a straw, please." Victoria Ash settled at the bar with a tired sigh. The evening was only half over, and already, she was at loose ends. Of course, being at an engagement party for two of your closest friends with neither your husband nor your working partner made it even more uncomfortable. The two situations were unrelated, at least.

The bartender gave her a friendly enough smile though. "The 12 year or the 15?"

She considered a moment. "The 15."

"Anything to eat? I could bring you the dinner menu."

"No, thank you." Victoria shook her head. She planned to have a quiet drink, then return to the event held in the adjoining hotel before any of her teammates missed her.

It was a special night, and for once, she wasn't overseeing security on the event. Tonight she was the guest of her longtime teammate and employer, Gabe Diaz. He and his fiancée, Maylin Chen, were celebrating their engagement. Any event hosted—and catered—by Maylin promised to feed the guests well, with exquisite innovation. There was absolutely no room left in Victoria's belly for the dishes this establishment had to offer.

Victoria had honored her hosts, eaten Maylin's fine cuisine, and had her fill of champagne. The last tiny dessert bite had been a delicate pear tart topped with impossibly thin shards of dark chocolate. With the decadent taste lingering on her tongue, the Dalmore was her choice to savor and then cleanse her palate. Perhaps after she'd finished a glass, or two, she'd have identified why she was in such an abominably irritable mood and be able to head back to the festivities in a better frame of mind.

Her drink was placed in front of her with the accompanying glass of plain water. She used the straw to transfer a drop of water into her scotch. Lifting the glass so she could enjoy the aroma from the amber liquid, she smiled as the tiny bit of water opened up the scotch to give her notes of winter spices and orange citrus along with richer hints of dark chocolate.

Yes. Given a few minutes to enjoy this and she would be in a much better mood. Her ex never did give her a moment's peace to enjoy her scotch. He preferred shots and chasers. Savoring a drink, enjoying the complexity a good scotch could offer, wasn't a preference of his. Now, she needn't take his hurried tendencies into consideration.

Wasn't that lovely?

"Why're we here?" A belligerent voice interrupted her enjoyment.

There'd been a handful of customers scattered through the establishment. These three had walked in from the street as she'd been ordering her scotch. Dressed in jeans and tees, they were probably looking for a different kind of bar. This one was a quieter place, enclosed on three sides with brick walls and hardwood shelves lined with real books. It invited people to come, sit, savor a drink and even enjoy a book. There'd been one or two people tucked into corners reading on e-readers. Besides being attached to the hotel hosting the event she'd been attending, the laid-back atmosphere of this bar had attracted her in the first place.

"You wanted good hard liquor." One of the noisy trio defended his choice at volume. "My app says this place is the best for scotch and whiskey. Good food too."

Belligerent Boy let loose a rude noise. "You know what, forget your stupid phone app. I saw The Five Point on TV. They've got drinks and food, plus we won't have to worry about them closing early. We can stay till breakfast. That's the kind of night I want."

Victoria kept watch on the trio without turning toward them. She could see just fine in the reflection on the floor-to-ceiling glass windows of the bar's street front. With luck, they'd take themselves out to the sidewalk in a minute and she could return her attention to her drink.

"I dunno. This place has something going for it. Saw some familiar faces maybe." The third pitched in at a more reasonable sound level, but he was still completely audible even from across the bar. "Gabe Diaz is here tonight for some event. You heard of him? Where he is, his team is too."

Sipping her scotch, she kept her glass raised to obscure part of her face. If she could see them in the reflection, they could turn and see her. Despite their careless words, they had been slowly turning to take note of the people in the room. None of their gazes had lingered longer than a second but they could've recognized her. Most people in her line of work made it their business to recognize another person in the private contractor field. It wasn't easy, but if they were familiar with Gabe then they'd have a chance at identifying her. She'd been with Gabe's team longer than any of her previous stints in the business.

She wasn't dressed for work though. It'd been a good time to wear the rose gown with the subtle golden shimmer, so sheer, it required a nude silk sheathe beneath. It fit her perfectly, the fabric poured over her torso to fall from her hips and pool into a fuller skirt around her ankles. She'd left her hair down for once. It hung free of the severe knot she kept it in for when she was working. A few soft curls worked well in her golden blond hair. Nothing about her shouted private security or former military.

"Ah, Diaz and his Safeguard experiment. Whatever." Belligerent Boy flopped his hand around in mockery. "Word is they aren't worth the contract fee. Clients aren't happy. If they're here, it's going to be a clusterfuck. Guaranteed. There are better companies to do the job."

She kept her expression neutral, but she filed the tidbit of information away. It would be wise to follow up and see if the comment had any validity to it at all. At the very least, Gabe would want to know it'd been said out in the bar.

His companions snickered. "Like yours?"

"Hey, I work for the best." Belligerent Boy raised his hands. "They appreciate good work and don't get their panties in a twist when a man heads out for well-deserved time off."

This was starting to sound like a badly scripted commercial. These men had walked into this bar on purpose. There was no way it was a coincidence. Yet, it had to be to pick a fight or stir up some similar ridiculousness. Real clients with serious contracts wouldn't be getting their information from bar gossip. On the other hand, journalists had been hanging around the Safeguard teams ever since Kyle Yeun had stood trial to testify against Phoenix Biotech. The trial had been right in the spotlight of public scrutiny, and Safeguard, specifically Lizzy Scott, had been his bodyguard. Perhaps Belligerent Boy was trying to score an interview with some journalist trying to get dirt. Either way, she'd best get them out of here before they cast a shadow on Gabe and Maylin's special night.

"Excuse me." The nice bartender had approached at this point, quite possibly at the worst moment. "If you gentlemen aren't going to order a drink or food, I'm going to have to ask you to head on to your next destination."

"Yeah?" That was a challenge. Belligerent Boy cocked his head to one side and threw out his chest. "You think so? You one of Diaz's wannabe real mercenaries, on watch at the perimeter? Maybe we should head inside and see how good Safeguard's security really is."

Actually, no. The bartender was simply doing his job. Since this event wasn't a contract, Safeguard wasn't maintaining high-level security. There shouldn't have been any need to. As far as anyone else was concerned, this event was a simple engagement reception. Victoria set her glass down, promising herself another scotch after this was resolved.

"Yeah nah bro, I reckon we take this outside." Another new voice had entered the mix, and this one had a wonderful accent. It wasn't British or European, closer to Australian but not a match for that continent either. Perhaps New Zealand?

"Who're you?" Belligerent Boy did seem to be looking for a fight.

"Does it matter?" The newcomer wasn't much taller than Belligerent Boy, but he managed to look down the few inches he had on the other man in a genial way. Truly, his broad shoulders and chest cut an impressive figure, and there was a strength of presence that filled available space in a way normal physicality could not. He took a few steps through the other three, forcing them to step aside before they thought to stand their ground, and headed outside.

The newcomer was ballsy.

Victoria would've been infuriated but she'd have been wary. The trio was the former and not the latter. They swarmed out after the man, probably as he'd intended. She followed at a more leisurely pace and gave the bartender a pat on the shoulder. "No need to worry for the moment. They'll all get this out of their system and move along."

Unless the four of them came through the glass, that was. The entire front of the bar and the adjacent hotel lobby was window front or glass door. Watching the three range out in a semicircle around the single man, they all appeared fairly capable to her experienced eye, a step above the average bar brawler at least. Someone could very likely come through the windows since it'd be better than throwing a man into the street where things could become much more fatal. First Ave wasn't the busiest of streets, but it still had traffic at this time of night.

A commotion on that scale would definitely require police and potentially disturb Gabe and Maylin's party. It wasn't something Victoria was willing to allow if she could help it, so she stepped out of the bar too.

They hadn't gone far, just out onto the sidewalk to stand under the nearest streetlamp. Unfortunately, it was one right in front of the lobby entrance to the hotel. Victoria sighed inwardly. Though perhaps it wouldn't turn out as bad as she was anticipating. The newcomer had turned to chat amiably with them, offering a pack of cigarettes.

Ugh. She truly disliked smoking. She could if she had to play a particular role for a mission, but she'd never taken up the habit of her own accord. However, it seemed to be an effective way to de-escalate the situation. She'd give the newcomer extra points for charm.

Belligerent Boy had shuffled forward as they chatted though, closing the space between him and the newcomer as they'd been lighting each other's cigarettes. Belligerent Boy turned to mutter something to one of his companions, bringing his hand near his mouth in an overly dramatic gesture of secrecy. They were all laughing but Victoria narrowed her eyes. His posture was awkward. His upper body twisted and his hips still squared up with the newcomer.

She pushed open the door and headed out of the bar. "Oy!"

The newcomer dropped his cigarette as she came out and bent to retrieve it. Belligerent Boy unwound at that moment, his upraised hand tightened into a fist, throwing a wild haymaker punch at the newcomer. Already low, the newcomer deepened his crouch and lunged at Belligerent Boy. He caught Belligerent Boy around the thighs, driving forward with his head and shoulder and hoisting the man in a considerable show of strength.

Belligerent Boy fell to the side, knocking one of his companions off balance as he went down. From Victoria's perspective, the collision might've saved Belligerent Boy from getting his skull smashed in on the corner of the lamppost. As it was, Belligerent Boy had the breath knocked out of him and hit the sidewalk.

It was still two on one, and this needed to end before hotel staff or someone on the street noticed the scuffle and called the police. Yelling again wasn't an option. Better to end it with as little noise as possible, and miraculously, the men had only uttered grunts in the few seconds since it'd started. She started forward toward the drunkard closest to her with her fists up, letting her heels clatter on the sidewalk with enough noise to get his attention.

Turned out, her target was a capable man in the middle of a fight. He heard her coming and turned to face her, taking a competent fight posture. She could slow down. Her gown and heels weren't optimal for confrontation, and he had a longer arm reach on her. He blinked slowly in the fraction of a second it took for her to consider, probably deciding the same thing about her appearance.

Screw it.

She rushed him instead, bending at the last possible moment to hoist her skirt and let loose a front kick instead of the punch he'd thought she'd been about to throw. She caught him in the chest but he had twisted slightly and managed to deflect some of the kick's force. Letting her momentum carry her into a turn, she pivoted low on both feet into a crouch and kicked out her other leg. He hadn't been prepared for her change in elevation, and her leg sweep caught him at the ankle. He fell flat on his back on the concrete with a whoosh as his breath left him.

In the meantime, the newcomer had managed to take the third man to the ground. With all three men groaning and gasping to catch their breath, her new friend grinned at her and stepped clear, offering her a hand up.

She reached into the front of her gown and pulled out a money clip. Tossing them a twenty, she sighed. "Why don't you boys go have a drink someplace else? It wouldn't be advisable to continue this…discussion. Police could be here any minute."

The newcomer at her side chuckled.

The three men scrambled to their feet, Belligerent Boy still dazed. Maybe he'd hit his head on the sidewalk after all. He paused, then grabbed the twenty. The trio headed down the street and around the corner.

"Well, that was less than subtle." Victoria slanted a look at the man next to her. "Your pack of cigarettes are crushed."

He glanced at the crushed pack where it lay forgotten on the pavement. "I hate the things anyway. Grabbed them up from one of the outdoor tables over here."

"Ah." She eyed her new ally as he straightened his clothing. "Are you all right?"

"All good, Queenie." Dark eyes twinkled with good humor, and the creases at the corners of his eyes spoke more of laughter than bad times. He ran his hand through his hair and managed to reestablish himself as quite presentable in fairly short order. "Thank you for the assist."

Come to think of it, she was in a much better mood after their brief scuffle. A workout, however unplanned, had done wonders for the tight ball of brooding she'd been carrying around recently. "I'll buy you a drink for defending the honor of Safeguard, if you'll leave off calling me Queenie."

"I don't know your name yet." He grinned, holding his hands open in a conciliatory gesture. "I only know you fight like a warrior dressed like a dream."

Pretty words delivered in a wonderful accent. She smiled despite herself. He noticed her give in and his grin widened. Oh, he was going to be the incorrigible type.

"Adam Hicks, at your service."

"I can wait outside, if you'd feel more comfortable." It was still early in the night, and while Adam was very interested in Victoria's company, he wasn't about to assume her coming up to his hotel room meant he was getting laid.

Of course, he wanted to. Very much. It'd been a long while and she was an incredibly attractive woman. He just wanted to give her every opportunity to give him clear signals. He'd invited her up here, though, on the premise of cleaning up her shoes and the bottom of her gown. They'd gotten messed up when she'd helped him encourage the other men to leave the bar downstairs. Apparently, she hadn't booked a room in this hotel for the Safeguard party.

"It was generous of you to offer the use of your sink. I wouldn't want to keep you out of your own room. It won't take me long to clean up." She gave him a sweet smile. Her face was striking with high cheekbones and an angled jaw. Her mouth was small, her lips plump. The effect was captivating.

He couldn't help but focus on those lips for a moment, wondering what she'd taste like. When he tore his gaze away and looked back up at her eyes, they were a steel blue and sparking with amusement.

Giving a relaxed smile in return, he held the door to his room open for her. He'd given her enough space to get by, but she brushed against him as she walked in anyway. A hint of warm, spicy perfume with a note of sweet teased him as her passing touch sent ripples of heat through his body. He swallowed hard and willed his cock to stay in his pants. He'd had the tuxedo fitted a few days ago, and he'd give the tailor points for having done the fitting to allow for good movement. He'd not torn a single seam in the fight earlier. But the cut and fabric of the pants were not going to hide the way he was responding to her.

Victoria paused, taking in the small but elegant hotel room. Her gaze noted the open closet and every nook and corner as she visually cleared the room, something he'd done as he'd opened the door and before he'd let her in. Her shoulders, bare in her lovely gown, relaxed a bit. She was in peak physical condition, without the sleek look of those who might remain slender by controlling diet. Muscles slid under her smooth, porcelain white skin in subtle definition. He'd not noticed earlier because her glorious blond hair had fallen in soft curls down her back. Now though, she'd pulled it over her shoulder.

She turned toward him, her gaze trailing as she took her time enjoying the look of the room. There she stood, framed in the light of the bedside lamp he'd left on, all rose and gold in the middle of an impeccably decorated room of creams, pale blues, and soft brown accents. He could be looking at a high-end magazine, really, or a dream. But he was awake and a very lucky man.

"I'll only be a few minutes." She crossed the room to the bathroom and left the door partially open.

He stepped inside and let the door close. This had been an unpredictable evening. He'd come on the last-minute invitation of the lead of the Safeguard Division. He'd had a chance to introduce himself to Gabriel Diaz, wish him and his fiancée well, and then have a few bites to eat as he'd circulated. The guests had been people both from Safeguard and the Centurion Corporation as well as close partners, including one or two representatives from local law enforcement. It'd been swank, the food was delicious, and the space somewhat crowded. He could blend in fine in those events but they drained him. He'd thought his cheeks would be sore from all the smiling.

Then he'd stepped out to the quieter bar for a drink and found himself a refreshing brawl, a little one, a breath of evening air. Ah, he was rough around the edges, what could he say? It'd been fun. And he'd met Victoria.

Who was now in his bathroom.

"Do you happen to have a safety pin or sewing kit?" Her voice was low-pitched and had a husky quality to it, but it carried well.

He headed for the closet and pulled his duffel off the floor. "Probably have both."

The duffel was more of a go bag containing enough clothing for the next few days, and he kept it equipped with simple travel necessities as well as spare ammo and extra blades. He was a private military contractor now, best to have whatever he might need on hand. Pulling out a small travel kit, he approached the bathroom door and held it out. "Here."

Victoria glanced up at the mirror, using the reflection the same way he was, to see around the edge of the door. "Thank you."

She opened the bathroom door a bit wider and took the kit from him. Her fingertips brushed the inside of his palm as she did, tickling him with the shock of their contact again.

"This gown was made to allow for dancing, not sparring." Her tone took on a wry flavor. "It's fine through the torso and the lower skirt, but the back, right at the bottom of the zipper, gave at the seam some. If I don't at least pin it for now, it could pull open even more, and I'll end up with unexpected air conditioning in this dress for the rest of the night."

He chuckled. "Did you need some help?"

She stopped twisting to see her back in the mirror and lifted her gaze to look at him via the reflection. "I guess that depends."

Her lids were at half-mast and lips pursed in a half smile. He stilled, waiting.

"How much longer am I going to be wearing this?"

Message received. He pressed the door to the bathroom the rest of the way open, and she watched him enter, giving him her back. He moved with care, not wanting to damage her dress and wishing he could tear it off her at the same time. It was slow torture for him to find the tiny zipper and pull it down, revealing more and more of her. She let the lace and silk slide to the floor in a puddle of pink-and-gold shimmer at her feet and sighed as he coasted his hands back up her sides to her shoulders.

She turned to him, lifting her face, her lips parted as she paused. "Just this, tonight, for fun. No strings attached. No surprises?"

He let his lips spread in a slow smile. "This is plenty surprise for me, Queenie, and I plan to keep my attention on exploring the adventure at hand. No strings. No ulterior motives. I'm just a very horny man right now."

Laughing, she smoothed the fabric of his tuxedo jacket, then grabbed the lapels in her fists. "Good. Let's have fun."

Chapter Two

A good fight to burn off Victoria's bad mood and a hot tumble to take the edge off the tight control she'd had on her emotions lately was perfect. She was a vigorous, single woman. If her ex didn't want her, fine. Adam obviously did, and so far, he'd proven to be both an excellent fighter and a polished gentleman. Now, she wanted all this delicious strength unclothed and all over her.

He hadn't answered her. Instead, he covered her mouth with his and sent her drowning in a very thorough kiss, only letting her up for air when she started to see stars behind her eyelids. His big hands gripped her waist and lifted her easily, setting her on the cool marble top of the bathroom counter. He pressed closer, coaxing her knees apart until his hips were settled between her thighs and his erection was snug against her.

She almost groaned. Oh, this was going to be good. Tugging at his tuxedo jacket, she managed to get it open and over his broad shoulders. Seriously, she could swing from them if she wanted. Once his arms were free of the jacket, he undid his cufflinks and untied his bow tie—a real one, she was delighted to see—and set those carefully aside before yanking off his tuxedo shirt.

Greedy for touch, she laid her hands on his well-defined abdomen. His skin was smooth and faintly tan with a copper undertone. He had a bodybuilder's physique, all glorious muscles. She ran her fingertips over the stark, black lines of the tattoo on the left side of his chest, fascinated by the grooved skin left by the complex design.

"Ta moko." His voice was gruff but there was no temper. Instead, there was a quiet pride. "Maori. Part of my heritage."

"Does it hurt?" She whispered the question as she leaned forward to brush her lips over the tattoo. She was drawn to the design, captivated, and turned on.

He didn't stop her. As she continued to explore his skin, he used his hands to wander over her shoulders and back, down the sides of her thighs and back up again. They continued to touch each other until her skin was so sensitive, she thought she'd cry. Then he cupped her ass and squeezed, hard.

She gasped, looking up at him, pressing her entire body against him.

His gaze was glazed with desire now, and he bent his head to her throat. His lips brushed her pulse, and the sound of her own breathing roared in her ears. He set his teeth against the soft spot where her neck met her shoulder, grazing her skin. She whimpered. When she'd ever made sounds like that, she wasn't sure, but he'd brought it out of her and she was feeling too good to worry about it. This time, when he kissed her, his tongue danced with hers.

His hands moved the entire time, petting her, his rough palms sliding over her skin and finding the most sensitive spots. As they kissed, he undid her bra and removed it. He cupped her breasts, squeezing one and rubbing his thumb over the sensitive nipple of the other.

She broke the kiss, gasping for air as he continued to play with her. He kissed and licked his way over her collarbone to her chest. His mouth closed over her neglected nipple first, wet heat and a sharp tug as his teeth gently caught her tight flesh. Trembling, she had to use both her hands to prop herself up on the counter, giving him free access.

And he took it. He licked and sucked at her breasts, alternating between one and the other. He took his time about it too, making sure to pay detailed attention to her responses and build on what he was learning about her body until she had her legs wrapped around his hips in need. The entire time, she'd had the hard pressure of his erection pressing against her with only their clothes keeping them apart.

"Not yet, Queenie." His voice had dropped so low, it sent shivers over her wet nipples.

He loomed over her for another kiss as he undid and dropped his pants. Then he was kneeling down in front of her, easing her panties off and keeping her perched on the edge of the counter.

"Can I taste?"

"Yes. Absolutely yes." She could've come up with

a more clever response, teased him maybe. But she wanted him to taste her. She wasn't about to be coy here.

He grasped the undersides of her thighs, pressing her legs apart and up. His tongue swept up through her aching flesh, and she cried out. He feasted on her then, sucking and licking, nibbling at her until all she could do was try to remember to breathe as the sensation drove her insane.

He released one of her legs and traced her opening with his fingertip, still tickling her clitoris with the tip of his very clever tongue. He pressed his finger inside of her, stretching her. It'd been a long time. She came around his finger, leaning forward to clutch at his shoulders as her inner core convulsed. He pumped his finger inside her, lengthening her orgasm until she calmed.

"Good. So good," he murmured.

She heard the distinct crinkle of a foil packet and blinked her vision clear to see him sliding on a condom. Good man, well prepared. She'd been about to ask, but now she didn't need to. She could focus on enjoying.

He stood and pulled her off the counter. Turning her around, he pressed her forward until she was bent over the marble. He reached forward and played with her breasts as he encouraged her to widen her stance.

"Look up." He straightened behind her and reached down between them. "Watch us."

He must've taken his erection in hand, pressing the tip of his penis against her. He slid it up and down her slit until she was panting, watching him wide-eyed and wanting him inside her. This was exactly what she needed and the way he was giving it to her was so very good. Her ex had never looked at her when they'd had sex, never wanted her to open her eyes. This was not her ex. She wanted to remember Adam.

This, this was intensely erotic, and the image of the two of them poised on the brink was enough to fuel her own fun for nights to come.

She arched her back and pressed her hips back in invitation, and he put his free hand on her tailbone as he slid into her. He stretched every muscle inside her as he entered, and she let out a happy groan as he did. The cool marble under her kept her steady, and she bit her lips looking up at him standing over her. God, he was beautiful.

He placed his hands on either side of her hips and started to move.

His abs rippled as he pressed his hips into her. First in a smooth rocking motion, easing in and out of her until she'd been able to take the full length of him. He made subtle moves, angling his hips to one side or the other as he continued. She couldn't tear her gaze from watching him, and the pleasure of it built inside her slowly, low in her belly as it was pressed against the cool marble. He changed his stance then, bending his knees and leaning forward a little, and the pressure of his penis inside her lit fireworks behind her eyes.

She cried out, almost screamed.

He chuckled, deep and dark and masculine. One hand coasted up her spine and grasped her hair, gently tugging, while the other took a firmer grip on her hip. He thrust then, harder and deeper, at the same angle.

"Yes. Don't stop. Yes." She was gasping, almost lost in the feel of him inside her. So, so good.

He picked up the pace, thrusting inside her hard and fast. Over and over, she called out as he drove her closer to the edge of sanity. Every muscle inside her tightened with the waves of sensation until she crested and came, clenching tight around him.

He shouted too, coming with her. He let go of her hair as he did, planting his hands on the counter, bracing himself over her as he convulsed. They remained like that for a long minute, their breathing ragged, until their heart rates came back down to something closer to normal.

He pulled out of her carefully and reached behind the bathroom door, retrieving a thick bathrobe and draping it over her where she still rested bent over the counter. Then he disposed of the condom and turned on the shower.

His dark gaze found hers in the reflection of the mirror. "Join me?"

She smiled.

Victoria entered her condo a few hours past midnight, disengaging the security. She deliberately ignored the packet of papers sitting on her desk in the living area and focused on doing a sweep to clear the space out of habit. Secure the area first. It might be overkill, especially considering her line of work had most recently evolved more into private security as opposed to the kind of contract work that made more enemies out in the world. But old habits developed for a reason, and it rarely did more harm to be careful.

She'd managed to survive a long time in a dangerous profession because she paid attention to details and didn't relax her exacting standards. There were, after all, other ways to relax.

Her heart rate kicked up slightly at the memory of Adam lying in the hotel bed, one muscular leg revealed by the tossed sheets. A night of sexual sport most definitely had her ready to unwind. He had tried to coax her into staying 'til dawn, but she hadn't wanted to linger beyond the warm aftermath of good sex. It'd been better to kiss him goodnight and head home.

She completed her check of the area in good spirits. Satisfied that her two-bedroom condo was empty of anyone but her and secure now that she was inside with locks engaged, she finally let her guard down. Even during her tryst with Adam, she'd been peripherally aware of her surroundings. Safety was a relative thing. The hotel room had been well and good for fun, but they'd both been very much awake. If something unexpected had occurred, she'd have been able to react. Here in her condo she could actually let go of consciousness and sleep.

Perhaps not peacefully, but professionals like her tended to gather disturbing memories. Nightmares weren't ever easy, and she woke in the middle of her sleep cycle more often than not, but she had to close her eyes and shut down for a few hours regardless.

First though, she wanted to savor the release of tension and indulge a bit. So she popped into the master bath and turned the taps to begin filling the tub. As the sound of running water echoed in the room, she dropped in a small bath bomb. The earthy fresh scents of mint and rosemary rose up with the steam.

She crumbled a soft chunk of a bath bar under the running water and watched for a moment as rich bubbles formed in the bath.

Leaving the tub to continue filling, she stepped out into her bedroom and slipped out of her gown. Her shoes went neatly into their storage cubby among a select collection of other footwear. Her wardrobe and accessories were limited, simply because she tended to travel light. Material belongings were things to be left behind in a rush. But what she did take the time to acquire was of good quality and versatile.

Her nose was sensitive, and now that she'd taken off her clothes, the slight musk of sex still clung to her. Her lips stretched wider in a satisfied grin. It'd been quite the romp and she had absolutely no regrets. All she needed now was a good soak followed by some liberal application of liniment to ensure her muscles weren't too stiff in the morning. Feeling brazen, she crossed her bedroom naked, returning to the master bath.

Stepping into the shower, she washed thoroughly. It was her preference to get every nook and cranny clean first, then settle in for a long soak. Visits to hot springs around the world were an interest of hers, and she'd picked up a few practices that'd made quite a lot of sense to her. Who wanted to soak while less than clean?

Her ex-husband did. Ugh. The man would jump into a pool covered in sweat and suntan oil. He'd never rinsed off first. Ever.

That's what chlorine is for, babe.

She shuddered and banished the voice of her ex, replacing it with the memory of golden brown skin under her fingertips. Adam Hicks was a spectacular encounter to take the place of past disappointments.

She stepped out of the shower and her bath was just about ready. Bubbles rose up and threatened to spill over the edge of the tub by the time she turned off the faucet. Cautiously, she slipped in one foot at a time. The water was hot—at the very threshold of what she could tolerate—which was exactly her preference.

Settling in and leaning back, she let the heat soak into her. It was a large tub, deep enough for the water to come up all the way over her shoulders. It'd been the main selling point that'd prompted her to buy this condo. There were plenty of lovely spaces available for sale or rent in the downtown Seattle area, but a tub this luxurious was hard to find anywhere.

To be honest, she hadn't been expecting the night to be so enjoyable. And it was about damned time she did have a worry-free, perfectly simple romp. It'd been exactly what she needed.

Stretching one leg at a time out of the water, watching the bubbles slide down her skin, she stifled a groan. Oh yes, this soak was not only an indulgent follow-up. It was a necessity.

Her new friend Adam knew what he was doing in bed, and the challenge of meeting him pleasure for pleasure would leave her sore everywhere.

Perhaps *friend* was farther than she wanted to take it. She was definitely inclined to think well of the man. He'd been fantastically responsive to her encouragements and considerate even as he'd sent them both out of their senses. But it wasn't likely that she'd run into him again unless both of them made an effort to contact.

Parties hosted directly by Safeguard like last evening were rare. If any of her colleagues attended formal events, it was on contract as some VIP's private security. While she'd guessed Adam was a contractor working with one of Safeguard's partners, she hadn't asked for details. She'd have to expend very deliberate energy to track him down. The same went for him in regard to her.

Neither of which was likely.

No. Her teammate Lizzy would've called this a hookup. And it'd been a good one. She settled her feet back under the water and just let the heat seep into her muscles. These were the kinds of nights she was looking for in between contracts. Just enough to release the sexual tension building inside her from time to time without any of the complications that came with clingy relationships.

Now, if she could convince Diaz to allow her to work solo rather than replacing Marc, her life would be just about where she wanted it.

A few minutes later, she rose out of the tub and took another quick rinse in the shower. Yes, it was repetitive. Indulging in self-care like this was a ritual of sorts with many steps of pampering. In all things, she liked to be thorough, detail oriented, and happy with the end result. Her ex had always lost patience with her, but he wasn't here to give her grief about this. Wasn't it lovely? Refreshed, she wrapped a thin satin robe around her frame and considered her very large, very welcoming bed.

"Tch." She sighed and headed back out to the living area.

If she tried to go to sleep now, which she was absolutely ready to do, the thought of the papers waiting on her desk would drive her right back out of bed. If there was one thing she disliked acutely, it was settling into a cozy bed with wondrous sheets and blankets then suddenly realizing you had to pee. This was going to be like that, but on the scale of realizing you had a urinary tract infection.

Picking up the papers, she reviewed them carefully, reading twice to be sure she understood the legal phrasing properly. It was bad news, again. But she wasn't surprised in the least. Her ex had been drawing out their divorce for ages now, and this was just the latest in a string of requests for evidence and excessive motions designed to tie up the official divorce proceedings ad nauseam.

She retrieved her smartphone and opened up her task-management app. Adding several tasks to her list for the coming day, she figured it was just as well her ex lived on the other side of the country. If she wasn't tempted to end this decisively, then one of her teammates might for the idiocy he insisted on putting her through. But that wasn't what the Safeguard team was about, nor their parent company, the Centurion Corporation.

Yes, they were a private contract organization. Mercenaries, to be blunt about it. But they did their best to do the right thing in every situation. They didn't succumb to petty impulses. The actions they took were decisive and strategic, making a difference in the bigger picture of reality.

Murdering her ex for being a buggering ass was a waste of their very elite skills.

All she wanted was for this divorce to be finished. Her relationship with him had been over and done years ago. At this point, he'd just been making things difficult out of spite. He was convinced that she owed him a higher standard of living than what he had without her. He'd been frustrated when she hadn't gone bankrupt paying the initial legal fees and simply taken his pathetic excuse for a settlement.

She made a respectable livelihood without him, thank you very much. Regardless of what poison he could spew about mercenaries for hire and about her in specific. All she wanted now was to be free of him, and he wouldn't give it to her. So the bastard could go rot as far as she was concerned. She'd continue this farce of a divorce process until he had no further resources to bring to bear.

It took minutes to scan the correspondence and store it digitally, then drop the originals to be filed away in offsite storage. She didn't feel peace of mind, per se, but she felt better knowing what the letter had been about and what steps she needed to take in the immediate future.

If there was one thing she hated, it was being caught up in a situation without having a plan to deal with it.

Chapter Three

"Morning."

Victoria crossed the small area at the back employee entrance to Safeguard and paused to lean in the doorway to Lizzy's office. "Good morning. Do any of us ever decide to take Sunday off?"

Working Fridays and Saturdays was actually fairly normal for them when it came to the brief, one-night private security engagements. Quite a few of the Seattle elite hired Safeguard to see to the security of their weekend appearances and social engagements. Sundays were less frequent and usually some of the resources could take the day.

"Apparently, there's an uptick in October weddings." Lizzy sighed. "Not that I'm complaining. There's something satisfying about snagging paparazzi and turning them away. Some of them are really creative about trying to sneak into people's personal space. It's not exactly a challenge, but I don't feel bad about keeping them out of people's lives."

Victoria raised her eyebrows. "We're doing weddings on a regular basis now."

Far stretch from the infiltration and surveillance missions they used to run in wilder places overseas. The environments had been much harsher and their objectives had been...less civilized.

"A select few." Lizzy pressed her lips together. "Celebrities and high-profile individuals experiencing threats. There's established proof of danger."

Fair. A target was most vulnerable at moments in their lives like wedding days. It would be the best day to do irreparable harm to them, either physically or psychologically. They'd live with the memory forever, if they survived in the first place. Another reason Victoria had absolutely no dreams of the perfect wedding.

Of course, an attack on any day was, by nature, unforgettable.

Nuptials. Parties. These were simple to oversee. A normal, civilian-staffed private security company could've been sufficient. Safeguard was being hired because they'd become fashionable. But the resources within Safeguard were experienced, highly skilled individuals. They were hired soldiers, all having served with one or more militaries in some of the most volatile environments around the world. To say they were overqualified for these contracts was ridiculously obvious.

"Is it just me?" Victoria considered her wording carefully. Lizzy had been a long-time teammate and one of the few people who could also be thought of as a trusted friend, but she was also second in command at Safeguard and they were in the office. "Or have we not been presented with the opportunity to stretch ourselves recently?"

Victoria had been with Safeguard from the beginning, earlier that year. Prior, she'd been a part of Gabe's fire team within the Centurion Corporation, the parent company. As part of Centurion, they'd seen plenty of action and every mission had been high risk. The objectives had been worth it though, and there'd always been a need to hone the skills they had.

When Safeguard had been created, it'd been a change of pace and a welcome respite, a different way of thinking and applying what she knew. Now, Victoria chafed at the lack of challenge.

The corners of Lizzy's mouth turned downward into a troubled frown, and the worry darkened her gaze. "Ever been warned to be careful what you wish for?"

Dark-haired, dark-eyed, she was lovely. Lizzy was the foil to Victoria's golden looks. The two of them had used their striking contrast to advantage in times past, when it'd been necessary to be the visual distraction. But Lizzy's forte lay in concealment and taking out her targets from a distance. She was a skilled sniper, one of the best Victoria had ever witnessed. To see Lizzy's calm disturbed was alarming.

"Something is churning," Lizzy offered slowly. "I haven't tracked it down yet, but Diaz is aware. There's hesitation out there to hire us, and we're not sure where it's coming from. Even our connections with Seattle law enforcement and the U.S. Marshals have seen some extra red tape."

Those connections were recent, a direct result of Lizzy's joint effort to provide protection for Kyle Yeun in the days leading up to his testimony in court against a huge biotech company called Phoenix Biotech. The mission had been successful. Both Seattle law enforcement and the U.S. Marshals had been interested in building stronger relationships for future collaboration. It seemed off for them to hesitate now.

"Interesting." Victoria pressed her lips together, thinking of Belligerent Boy's commentary from the prior evening. Reputation was key among private contract organizations. Safeguard might be new, but they had the backing of Centurion Corporation for the time being. And Centurion was recognized as one of the best in the business, providing expert resources forged in the world's most challenging environments to fulfill military defense contracts around the globe.

The Safeguard Division specialized more in private protection. They were elite-level bodyguards. They should have been guarding high-profile individuals where local law enforcement or government oversight could not. Instead, they were watching over…weddings.

"We're still in proof of concept." Lizzy was likely to have followed the same line of thought Victoria had, perhaps had been going over it for longer. "Centurion can back us for a while, but we need to be in the black and established in the first two years to prove out our value. It's one thing to build a reputation from scratch, slow and steady. It takes way longer to repair a tarnished rep. It's not worth the investment for Centurion when they can pursue other potential divisions."

While Centurion was a good employer, it was also run by shrewd businessmen. They'd cut Safeguard if it didn't prove out. Victoria wasn't sure she wanted to remain with Safeguard for the long term, but she wanted it to be her choice. Besides, there were people out there who needed Safeguard or an entity like it. Without them, Maylin Chen might be dead and her younger sister still missing. Kyle Yeun wouldn't have survived, his sister and nephew either sent back to South Korea or lost in the system here in the United States. Safeguard needed to exist. It was more a matter of finding those clients, the ones who had a real need…and the funds to hire them.

Even as she thought about it, Victoria recognized the whimsy in it. There were always people in need. There were even television shows and movies about soldiers of fortune helping them. But in reality, money was a harsh limiting factor.

"If you hear anything specific from your contacts about the perception of Safeguard, let us know," Lizzy said finally. Every professional in the private sector of the military defense and private security industry had contacts. A solid information network lasted beyond any finite contract or job with a specific organization. It was a lifelong resource. "Could be nothing but it's probably something. We can't afford to be caught by surprise. And to be honest, we've been due for a few professional challenges with the jump start we had."

Victoria huffed out a laugh. It went unsaid, but two names came to mind: Edict and Phoenix Biotech. Twice now, Safeguard resources had clashed with Edict, the competing private contract organization backed by Phoenix Biotech. And both of those times, Safeguard had deprived Phoenix Biotech of very valuable targets.

"Corporate competition is not my area of expertise." Victoria shook her head. She didn't have the patience for the subtlety it required. Give her a straightforward plan of action any day as opposed to being trapped in a boardroom over business negotiations, pretending to be civil.

"We leave that to minds like Kyle's." Lizzy nodded, though the softness around her mouth and eyes was reserved solely for when she was thinking of her lover. "He says they could be undercutting us to take up all the contracts in our business sector."

"There are always more contracts." At least, in the years Victoria had been a private specialist, there had been. Sometimes it meant moving to a new hot spot. Other times, it meant compromising ethics for continued work. So far, she'd only ever had to slightly bend her own rules on the latter.

The trick to surviving in the business was to keep in mind that tomorrow could always push you harder than you've been *so far*.

"In any case, listen for whispers in your network. Both Diaz and I agree this is just the symptom of whatever is going on." Lizzy rolled her shoulders. "We're going to keep having growing pains as we get better established, and we need to be able to handle them quickly."

"Lovely." Victoria was only too glad it was Lizzy dealing with all of these considerations alongside their CO, Diaz, and not Victoria. She preferred to tackle her challenges project by project. "Speaking of growing pains, I came in to meet with Diaz about a new contract."

Please let it not be a wedding.

"And a new partner." Lizzy grinned. "Standard operating procedure. We work in pairs now, and your new partner is waiting in the reception area. Why don't you go get him and bring him back to Diaz's office. I'll track down Diaz for you."

It was the new standard operating procedure she didn't want to follow. If she could convince Diaz to let her work solo, she'd be much more likely to stay on a while longer. She hadn't broached the possibility with either Diaz or Lizzy, but her thoughts had been leaning toward whether to stay or go often since Marc had been injured. She needed to consider the options more first and define for herself what her deciding factors were going to be.

She straightened and started to step away, then turned back. "You look too happy over this situation."

Lizzy's eyes widened. "Who, me? Let's just say that dating within the company hasn't been addressed by HR yet."

"There's no conflict of interest," Victoria responded automatically. "You and Kyle have very different positions here."

Kyle was a program manager and head of finance for Safeguard. His was a desk position. The chances of him going out in the field with Lizzy, and their relationship endangering a mission, was slim to none. That said, at one time, Kyle had been out there with only Lizzy to keep him alive. So he had an appreciation for what the rest of them did, when they weren't covering social events.

"Not talking about me here." Pushing away from her desk, Lizzy rose and came around to lean her hip on the edge. "You haven't looked twice at the recent new hires. But this one? He's the type to stand out. If I know you, and I do, this one is the one that'll put your panties in a twist."

Victoria snorted. Maybe if she hadn't had a chance to feed a certain need the prior evening, she'd be more curious. "Whoever he is, he's a potential partner. That would be a definite conflict of interest. You should not be flirting with that kind of mess as an administrative."

Lizzy shrugged. "This is me, talking to you as a friend. It might be a good thing to make room in your life for something other than work and lame friends like me."

Ah, but Victoria was still cleaning up the mess of removing past mistakes from her life. Work and true friends were dependable. She needed them. What she didn't want was any more messy, complicated, painful holes in her world.

"I have what I need." Victoria gave Lizzy a smile. "No worries. There's a certain satisfaction to being free to wander if I like."

"So long as you don't wander away from Safeguard, I'm good. It'd be a staffing headache."

It was a possibility. All their agreements with Safeguard and the Centurion Corporation could be terminated at will from either side. Victoria opted not to voice the thoughts she'd been having yet.

"I promise I'll train my replacement." It was an old joke between her and Lizzy.

"For now, just work on training your new partner." Lizzy pulled a tablet from her work surface and held it out to Victoria. "Take this with you too. It's his agreement to read and sign."

Victoria took it without another word, just a chuckle, and headed down to the reception area.

"Great space, but where's the coffee?" Adam muttered.

He'd reported in on time this morning and had been instructed to wait. He had. Plenty of his time in the military had been a cycle of hurry up and wait, so it was nothing new. But he was downright knackered from the night prior. "I could use a cuppa coffee for sure."

He'd have thought such a new, obviously well-thought-out office space would have a kitchen area for its employees. After all, Safeguard Division was located in a new or close to new corporate center, taking up the entire floor of a six-story building.

The wide-open office space gave him line of sight across a majority of the floor, in point of fact. There were no cubicles to carve out space for poor bastards trapped at a desk for the main portion of their waking hours. Instead, clusters of comfortable chairs and table spaces had been placed around the space, welcoming discussion and maybe collaboration.

Small rooms or pods lined the interior, but the walls were all glass for complete transparency. They were places to find privacy but not to hide. The glass also allowed natural light in from the floor-to-ceiling win-

dows on the outer walls, offering sweet as views of El-
liot Bay, Puget Sound and the Olympic Mountains. It all
depended on which side of the building he was facing.

It was a high-tech atmosphere he could appreciate,
with a touch of class in the design. He could be as rough
and ready as any soldier out there. It didn't mean he
didn't appreciate a space conducive to productivity.

Scattered across the floor, employees were working on laptops, sitting or standing at adjustable work-
stations. There were even treadmill desks scattered
here and there. It seemed like too big a space for so
few people, but Safeguard's business meant its key assets weren't in the office. Those visible here were more
likely support staff.

There was the slightest sound of steps around the
corner, the one blind corner in the place. The fact that
it was on the approach to the reception area was no
accident. "Mr. Hicks. I'm sorry to keep you waiting."

Gabriel Diaz stood waiting as Hicks rose. Diaz was
dressed in jeans and a black polo, neat and relaxed at
the same time. The man's build was solid. The leader of
Safeguard hadn't gone soft spending time in the office.

"No worries." Hicks took Diaz's offered hand in a
firm shake. "Thank you for inviting me to your special
night last evening. Being new and all, I'm not properly
one of the team yet."

He watched Diaz closely. Safeguard wasn't the first
organization he'd spoken to on returning from New
Zealand, ready to work. He'd initially reached out to
one or two smaller groups that'd accepted other men
from his unit. There'd been a strange tension in those

talks, even with the mates he'd served with back when they'd all been active US military. He'd eased carefully away from those opportunities, wary of the way his former squad mates had been toward him. Considering how he'd left active service, he shouldn't blame them. Maybe. But he'd hoped they'd have remembered his good years, at least been willing to give him the chance to overwrite the one last mission.

No. The memory of the last had been in their eyes. It'd erased trust and left him with cold greetings on his return. So here he was at Safeguard, starting fresh.

But Diaz was completely relaxed, no sign of wariness or awkwardness. "My fiancée tells me food and drink are an important part of team building. You're going to be a part of my team, so it made sense to give you the chance to meet and mingle with our people and our partners from the beginning."

No mention of the scuffle in front of the hotel. Diaz might be aware of it. He might not. Hicks decided it best not to mention unless his new employer did. It wasn't something to boast about, and defending the honor of his new team shouldn't be something he needed to tell everyone he'd done. It was just something a good person did.

Hicks grinned and nodded. "Fair. I'm eager to get started."

Diaz cocked his head to the side slightly. "I think your partner's arrived. She's probably headed down the hall now. Might get delayed checking in with my second."

She. "I'll be honest, sir, I've got no issue with female counterparts. Met some skilled professionals in the business. But I've never been partnered directly with a lady. Any tips you have on how to get off to a positive start would be much appreciated."

Diaz had gone still when Hicks started talking, but by the end, one of Diaz's eyebrows twitched. "Up front and honest is always good. Treat a lady as an equal is a given or you'd be better suited for other organizations. Remember, she's a proven member of the team. You are still on probation."

Hicks set his jaw and nodded. No argument there. When he'd made the decision to enter private contracting, several of his inquiries had been met with cold reception and immediate rejection, even though none of those had been mates he'd served with or anyone who'd know him personally. Those should've been neutral opportunities. He'd been surprised. The terse responses hadn't been accompanied with explanations, but he'd expected his experience would've landed him more direct interviews than he'd gotten. At least a chance to present himself as a person beyond the service record.

He'd need to reestablish a network of contacts in the industry now that he was back. Then he could look into why. In the meantime, Safeguard and Centurion Corporation had been his best option. Any other options were outfits with reputations for shadier ethics. He'd have been faced with the same impossible choices that'd driven him out of active duty in the first place.

He had a chance here to build a new career. Proving himself first was fair. He just had a feeling there were marks against his name already, and there shouldn't be.

His last mission on record should've been buried under so much need to know, no one would've bothered to dig for it. Even then, the truth wasn't necessarily reflected in the report.

"Why don't we wait for her in my briefing room. All the conference pods are taken. She'll find us and join us." Diaz motioned toward a wall of glass.

Adam jerked his head in an affirmative and cleared his head of the past. It wouldn't be constructive here and now. As they walked, the frames of glass doors were visible at regular intervals. Each of the "pods" was separated by equally transparent walls with a horizontal strip of frosted treatment across the middle sections to provide privacy while still giving line of sight from the knees down for anyone inside those pods. People could conduct business in those small conference rooms without feeling like they were in fish bowls, but it was still easy to tell if there was anyone in those rooms.

In many ways, the entire office was set up to suit professionals who maintained a level of hypervigilance. The layout was wide-open, maximizing visibility to everything in the main area. Diaz paused at a door toward the end of the line, and Adam glimpsed around the corner to a whole different area of office space. Maybe that's where they were hiding the coffee.

Diaz opened the door and stepped inside, holding it for Adam to follow. This room was different. Multiple screens were set up and synched with a camera to support videoconference. As they moved to sit at the table, Diaz touched a control panel set on the wall, and the clear walls turned opaque. Nice.

"My office is connected to this briefing room." Diaz tilted his head to indicate another closed door. "When you are here, you are welcome at any time so long as I'm not in a meeting with someone else."

"You don't have an admin dragon guarding the entrance to your office?" Adam bit the inside of his cheek. Not everyone appreciated his humor, and it might be too early to test it on his new employer.

Diaz snorted. "I'll need to find one eventually. It takes a specific type of dragon to deal with my people. I don't want them turned away for the sake of a booked calendar, and for the most part, they'd walk right over a normal admin."

There was a brief knock and the door from Diaz's office opened.

"I cut through. Hope you don't mind." The new voice was oddly familiar, unmistakably feminine with a low, husky quality to it.

Adam stood and kept his face carefully neutral as he looked into her electric-blue gaze.

Diaz rose as well. "Victoria Ash, meet your new partner, Adam Hicks."

Chapter Four

"So, how have you been?" Adam cleared his voice and shifted awkwardly in the passenger seat. "Since last night?"

Victoria counted to ten, considering the various things she could say. Ultimately, she discarded pleasantries and got straight to her immediate thoughts. "You didn't tell me you worked for Safeguard."

Adam didn't bristle defensively as she'd expected. Instead, the big man relaxed. "Technically, I didn't. Not last night. Today is my first day. I try not to claim what isn't yet true. A man never knows what can happen from one day to the next."

His relaxed attitude and easygoing manner had been attractive to her last night. Today, she hadn't decided if it amused her or irritated her. Perhaps a mix of both. It remained to be seen whether he could seriously apply himself to an actual contract.

"Cutting it a bit fine, aren't you?" She eased her grip on the steering wheel. He hadn't put up a fight about which of them was going to drive once they'd left Safeguard headquarters. Which was a good thing because she needed a measure of control over the current situation to regain her composure. "You are coming perilously close to a lie by omission."

Negotiating the stop-and-go traffic of downtown Seattle meant driving was going to be tedious until they reached the ferry. Then it was going to be concentrated wait time. Giving him the silent treatment the whole way didn't appeal to her. She also had no idea how to move forward in any kind of constructive way. She was still too caught up in what he hadn't told her.

"Honest truth: I didn't intend to mislead you." He held out his hands, palms up within her range of sight. "I was very interested in where we were headed last night and figured to deal with tomorrow's problems when they presented themselves. It was a very enjoyable night. I hope you agree."

Oh, it'd been lovely. She wasn't going to erase the memory of it with any sort of denial. "Tomorrow is now today, though. And this is a problem."

"You didn't argue with Diaz." Adam's tone had gone quiet, sober. The warm geniality suddenly missing unsettled her.

"No." She drew out the response as she considered her own reaction. "I decided to follow your lead in the introductions. I wanted the chance to talk to you first before I asked him to rearrange his plans for the current contracts."

Adam was silent for a moment. "Does Safeguard have that many? Seems to me, Diaz would listen if you had a problem with working with me."

Victoria lifted a shoulder. "Contracts are coming in

and our resources are spread to capacity to cover while we bring on new people like you. Diaz would listen, but I don't raise issues until I'm sure I know what I want and have a mitigation plan to propose. I still need to work out what I'd propose from two aspects."

No one appreciated problems, but it was important to identify them early. She disliked people who only found them, though. That sort tended to dump issues into someone else's lap and walk away having washed their hands of any responsibility. If a person was intelligent enough to anticipate a problem, they could exercise the intellectual effort to come up with a few possible solutions too.

"And what are those two aspects?" His words had a hint of humor back in them.

Tension between her shoulder blades eased in response. That neutral tone of his was something to watch for in the future. In some people, it was a lack of commitment or intelligent response. Adam Hicks was neither, and she had a hunch it hid quite a lot going on inside his mind.

"For one thing, I don't see a reason to refuse to work with you outright. It took me by surprise, yes, but there hasn't been any indication we wouldn't be able to partner well. Quite the opposite, actually." Well, depending on how one decided to take the wording there. She refused to glance in his direction. He had a way of smiling, slow and devilish. It would be far too distracting at the moment. "The second consideration would be the current contracts. I would much rather take on this situation than oversee security for another wedding."

He laughed then, loud and unfettered. It filled the car with his energy and lightened the mood. "You could've asked to have me booted to a different job."

She shook her head slightly. "If I'd decided to protest an assignment, it should've been me to go to a new one."

"Thank you." His gratitude was expressed simply and with sincerity.

It shouldn't keep her off balance, but it did. Most of the people she'd encountered in her line of work didn't express things like appreciation or thanks easily. It was awkward at best, avoided more often than not. It could be considered a weakness, something to be taken advantage of down the line. If you admitted thanks, then a person could claim you owed them. There were less than half a dozen people in the world she'd give such an advantage to. From where she was sitting, Adam had a lot of self-confidence in being able to utter those two words.

"Glad you decided to keep me on for this one," Adam continued. He tilted his seat back a few inches and put his hands behind his head. "This is looking to be an easy job, aye?"

"Tch. This is not going to be easy. Did you listen during the briefing?" As much as she loved his Kiwi accent, she could swear it got stronger just then.

"I did." He continued to sound unconcerned. "We're enhancing the security on a private home, both physical and IT, then training his personal security team on the systems we've put into place. Definitely easy. It's a house, not a compound."

"A private home in the middle of a residential area

is more difficult. Neighbors make things complicated. Too many innocent bystanders walking around tripping alarms to snoop over their neighbor's wall." Victoria sighed. It'd been less than an hour, and her blood pressure was already up. "There are no easy jobs. Take this seriously. Do it right, with every attention to detail."

"Easy there. I hear you." Adam sat up in his seat.

His change in posture helped ease her irritation, but she still shot him a dubious sideways glance.

"I do my job and I do it well." His voice had turned serious again. "I'm also very good at what I do. To me, this is looking to be a straightforward couple of months. It means a lot to know we don't have an anticipated body count."

True. She'd been a part of enough operations where things like chance of survival and potential body count were unspoken assumptions. They might be briefed on those specifically or it might go unsaid. It depended on the briefing officer. Compared to those remembered missions, yes, he had a point. This job had a different level of difficulty.

She pulled the car in line and glanced at her watch. They'd made it in good time. "Line's short. A few minutes now and we'll be on the ferry. Perfect timing."

He didn't press the earlier line of discussion. It made sense. She'd been the one to bring it up. Instead, he leaned forward to look beyond the cars ahead of them. "How long is the crossing?"

She considered. "Thirty to forty minutes, I think?"

"Huh. How long would we have waited if we'd missed this one?"

"Between forty-five and sixty minutes." She checked her smartphone for the schedule just to be sure. The weekend schedule differed from the weekdays. He didn't respond but the weight of his regard pricked her temper again. "What?"

"You are a very detail-oriented woman." There was no mockery in his words. Actually, he sounded quite sincere, and the heat in his gaze was appreciative.

As soon as they pulled the car onto the ferry, she was stepping out of the car. It was getting too damned hot in here and they still had business to discuss. "I am and we need to work out another detail."

He cocked his head to the side, one eyebrow raised in query.

"Last night." Was amazing. But she didn't say what he already knew. Cocky bastard. "Didn't happen."

His eyes closed and reopened in a slow blink. The warmth leached from his face, and the smile faded until his expression was completely neutral.

"We are partners now." Her reasoning was sound. She was sure of it. "We need to be able to work on a professional level. Intimacy complicates things and puts our quality of work at risk."

"And we can't have that." He wasn't happy, but he didn't sound angry or sad either. Instead, his words were flat.

"Absolutely not." It hurt, the way his easy camaraderie had been stuffed away somewhere. She wanted it back. Which was childish. This was for the best. "Diaz doesn't know, and no one needs to ever take it into consideration. We can just put it behind us and build a professional working relationship."

She stopped talking then and waited for his response. The cars ahead of them moved forward, and she eased their car onto the ferry in line with the rest. It wasn't until the ferry was on its way across the Puget Sound that Adam answered her.

"Sweet as."

"Excuse me?"

He shrugged. "Means 'okay.' Sweet as. I'll take your lead on this. Once we build a working relationship, we'll revisit this discussion about what else is between us. Yeah?"

"No."

Hadn't he said something like "yeah, nah" last night?

He grinned. "Now you're sounding like you might be confused."

Yes. She scowled at him. "No, we are not revisiting."

He leaned toward her, not intimidating, just coming right into her personal space. Her heart kicked in her chest, and she had the urge to grab hold of his shoulder, his arm, any part of him.

He didn't come closer though. Instead, his gaze caught hers. "There is this between us. I like it. You have a point about our working together professionally. We'll get there. Then we'll come back to this. If you don't want it then, I'll back off. But I won't pretend it never existed."

"When I forwarded the signed statement of work to Mr. Diaz yesterday, I hadn't anticipated he would send his team on a Sunday." Roland Edwards folded his arms across his chest and made no move to open the iron gate blocking the entrance to the drive. "I'd assumed work would begin the next working day, not literally the next afternoon."

Adam stood next to Victoria as their new client glowered at them both and decided to let her do the meet-and-greet niceties. His sense of humor had a tendency to tick off men like Edwards. Well, Adam also seemed to have a knack for riling up Victoria, but stirring up her temper was irresistible.

"We apologize for disturbing you on your weekend, Dr. Edwards, but it was our understanding that you wanted to start immediately. The statement of work also indicated work to progress on weekends whenever possible to bring in the timeline." Victoria's tone was low and soothing, but there was a no-nonsense edge underlying the softness.

Dr. Edwards took a long, steadying breath and dropped his arms to his sides. "Yes. You are correct. I apologize for my sharpness. I've been unsettled recently, and it is good for you to start right away for my peace of mind. Why don't you both come inside the grounds? And call me Roland. When you say Dr. Edwards, I look around for my father."

It took effort not to raise an eyebrow. Roland was well into his late forties and an independently wealthy entrepreneur. Yes, he had a PhD in something. Adam didn't remember exactly what. But Roland Edwards had made his fortune investing in small ventures, startup companies, not in academic research. He didn't seem the type to be looking over his shoulder for his father.

"Where is your security team?" Victoria had stepped inside the now-opened gate, watching it retract to one side automatically.

The gate opened slow to admit visitors on foot or wide enough for a vehicle to come up the longer drive-way. It could and did stop midway and reverse to close once Adam had come within the grounds. Adam con-sidered the speed and mentally timed it as it closed after him. It wasn't going to be crushing anyone by accident. "Can this gate be locked closed?"

"Of course." Dr. Edwards—Roland—sounded some-what defensive.

Adam gave Roland his best friendly-but-professional smile. He'd save the real grins for Victoria. "No time like the present to start asking the questions we'll need to redesign your security."

The corner of Roland's mouth quirked in transient response. "Indeed. Why don't I take you for a walk of the grounds then, while my security team prepares to meet us."

"Is it standard practice for you to answer the gate?" There was an edge to Victoria's question this time, and Adam wondered if Roland had an issue with answering questions from women.

It wouldn't be the first time a woman like Victoria had to deal with testosterone-poisoned brains. Adam figured it'd be best—and safest—to let her handle it her own way. He'd be ready to back her up if she needed it, but if he read her right, she'd be establishing the way of things fairly quickly.

Fortunately, Roland seemed to pull himself together. "I owe you answers to two questions, don't I? I was in the middle of something when you arrived, and I admit I am still distracted. To your first question, the security team has a small building separate from the main house. They monitor the grounds but have instructions to remain as unobtrusive as possible. Unless they are needed to respond to an emergency, I wanted to be able to traverse my own home as if they aren't here. They are most assuredly watching us."

Victoria nodded. Otherwise, her face was a pleasant mask of polite attentiveness. There were no lines on her forehead or around her eyes to give away amusement or worry or temper. "A good foundation but I had the impression you have need for enhanced security. We may have to revise your current instructions."

Roland's lips pressed together. "Yes. As necessary."

"We'll discuss each change with you prior to implementation." Her calm assurance was impressive but Roland's shoulders were tightening. "We want to be sure any changes are explained so you feel comfortable inside your home."

"Safety is the primary objective." Roland's voice had grown taut with anxiety. "It is my habit to answer my gate personally when I am available. That may have to change. I am a private man and I have made enemies in business. It's become clear I've need to take serious measures. If I need to sacrifice convenience or comfort to ensure this property becomes impenetrable, then we will make the necessary changes. I appreciate the offer to include me in the process, but if my approval should become a bottleneck to what you as the experts see as a critical need, do it first and explain to me after."

Victoria smiled finally, a genuine and breathtaking expression lighting her entire face. "Understood and agreed. Let's walk the perimeter of your property, then, and see what we have to work with at the moment."

She turned to a security camera installed at the top of the pillar framing the gate. Leaning forward slightly, she peered directly into the camera and made a beckoning gesture with her hand.

"I imagine that should summon someone out to meet us." She straightened and turned to them. "Shall we go?"

Roland paused. "I always run a reference check on any vendor or services provider. Initially, the references for Safeguard Division and Centurion Corporation were impeccable. The negotiations for the statement of work were very quick by necessity, a matter of days. In the same timeframe, one or two of my references noted a change in the reputation of Safeguard, with the ability to fulfill your contracts in question. They hadn't experienced the issues themselves, but felt the need to warn me of the risk." He stared hard at Victoria. "Is Safeguard capable of honoring our contract and keeping not just me, but my entire household and property safe?"

Victoria didn't blink. "Yes."

Chapter Five

"You have a lovely estate." Victoria meant it. It was beautifully landscaped with an eye for privacy. The hedges and trees would foil any snooping, law-abiding citizens who wouldn't think of actually trespassing. In normal circumstances, it would be more than sufficient for an eccentric, wealthy homeowner. The level of security indicated as necessary in the statement of work and the acute anxiety her new client was projecting hinted strongly toward serious issues though.

Whether they were in his mind or tangible might not be a concern. Or they could be. She'd treat them as real in any case, because the new security design would be most effective that way.

"Well, you've seen just about the whole of the property at this point." Roland came to a stop once they reached the back of his grounds facing Eagle Harbor. He even had a small dock, extending out into the harbor with a deck boat and a few kayaks at the end. Directly across the harbor was the ferry terminal where they'd arrived. "What do you propose?"

Adam shifted his weight and turned his head, ostensibly to look out over the harbor. She thought he might be hiding a grin.

"We haven't seen everything yet." She kept her voice level and upbeat. "We've only walked along the one side of your property from your front gate to the back here. You've been very helpful telling us about your neighbors on each side and some of the history of your estate. Next, we'll want to walk the full perimeter. Then we'll do another, slower walk and take pictures of everything. We'll do the same around your actual house and any other buildings. Then we'll work our way from the inside of those buildings outward."

Adam had been capturing images as they walked with his smartphone. He'd been so discreet, she thought Roland might not have noticed as he'd been engaged in conversation with her. She approved. No need for the client to be caught up in all the details of their work.

Roland opened his mouth to say something but what they heard was a sharp bark.

Adam coughed into his fist as they all turned to see a low-set, sturdy dog running toward them on very short legs. Mostly black, the dog had accents of tan with white splashed down its chest and paws. Its erect, triangular ears and tapered muzzle gave it a fox-like expression. Following behind the little dog was a group of four men.

These were likely to be Roland's existing security team. Now was as good a time as any for them to get a good look at each other. All cut from the same cloth, fit and crossing ground with an economy of movement. They ranged in age from silver fox to Adam's age. In fact, one of them was staring hard at Adam.

"Not a place I expected to see you, Hicks!" the man called out.

Adam chuckled. "The world is full of weird coincidences. That's for sure. What are you doing out in the wops?"

"The what?" The other man's face twisted with confusion and a shadow of something uglier, there and gone again as soon as Victoria blinked. "Man, you went native on your trip down under."

"I spent time with family in New Zealand, bro, not Australia." Adam's smile faded a fraction and his jaw tightened.

"Same difference, right, *mate*?" The other man laughed. The rest of the security team remained relaxed but didn't join in their teammate's amusement.

Kiwis didn't particularly like being grouped in with Australians, if Victoria remembered correctly. The sentiment was mutual to her understanding. They had a somewhat amicable rivalry going in many aspects of culture, most especially sports. This man had an East Coast, US accent. Perhaps he wasn't particularly…global.

The little dog had reached them, coming to a skidding halt next to Roland. It appeared to sit next to their client, but it was a bit hard to tell. His legs were so short, his rump only sank down a couple of inches, and with the grass around the dock high enough to brush the dog's belly, well, she was fairly certain the dog was sitting. Panting, the dog regarded her with what looked like a smile and a lolling tongue, his dark eyes full of intelligence and genial interest. Ah well, always a plus to have a well-behaved dog on the property. This one might not be particularly built for intimidation, but it had better hearing and sharper sense of smell than humans. It would be worth the effort to get to know the dog's habits so the security team could note if the dog sensed something out of place.

Roland sighed and stooped to give the little dog a scratch at the shoulders. "This is Tegan. He lives in the main house with me."

"Head of security, aye?" Adam laughed and knelt to hold out his hand in a loose fist for Tegan to sniff.

Tegan stretched his neck and sniffed Adam's knuckles. Then the little dog stood and approached, his butt wiggling. Victoria guessed his tail would be wagging, if the dog had a tail. Instead, he had a nub denoted by a heart-shaped patch of tan fur at his hind end. Once the dog seemed to have greeted Adam to his satisfaction, she knelt down to make acquaintance as well.

He really was a cute dog.

"So you're the consultants here to give this place an overhaul?" Adam's acquaintance had approached in the meantime with the rest of the security team. His tone was friendly enough, but there was an edge underneath his words. This man was not going to be a champion for the upcoming changes.

Victoria straightened to face them. Her toes warmed in her shoe as Tegan promptly sat on her foot. She decided to leave him there. "Yes."

The man gave her an assessing once-over. It started out professional and turned into blatant interest quickly. "Pleasure to meet you."

Sure.

Luckily for the man, Roland stepped in and made introductions. Dante had the lead with the most experience in private security. The man was aging well and his silvering hair suited him. His weathered skin had the look of a perpetual tan, a contrast in the Seattle area where there weren't enough sunny days. He'd worked for Roland for about a decade and held his position both based on seniority and continual efforts to maintain knowledge in up-to-date security concepts.

"If you have any questions, I'd be happy to sit down and provide whatever information I can." Dante met her gaze and held it, then looked at Adam in turn as he spoke. It was good of him to include them both in his offer. She could appreciate the career the man had built for himself and respected his continued development. Many others might let themselves get comfortable, stagnate.

Ray and Brian were close partners.

"Hey."

"Yo."

Neither of them was much for words but they each gave her a solid handshake. The former was a stocky man with sandy-colored hair and eyes, who looked like his fair skin would burn on the few sunny days Seattle did get. Brian was quite possibly the largest Chinese American she'd ever met, built like a hockey player with no need of the protective gear. The two of them seemed to trade wordless cues. A nod here, and look there, the unspoken communication tended to result in grins between the two of them as they shared a private joke. Close friends for certain, though she didn't get the impression of a more intimate relationship. She didn't particularly care if they had one, but it was good to be able to take any relationships into consideration when assigning shifts.

Adam's acquaintance, Jay, was the newest addition to the team. In fact, he'd only joined in a few days prior. Apparently, Roland had decided to expand his personal staff in addition to hiring Safeguard.

"However I can be of help, don't hesitate to let me know." Jay kept his focus on Victoria, but his gaze wasn't directly meeting hers. Instead, he seemed to be looking at her forehead or her nose. If he could've gotten away with it, she was sure he'd be staring at her breasts. He'd taken his time looking her up and down a moment earlier.

He had auburn hair, pale skin under a fading tan and hazel eyes. He was attractive enough but the way he tended to wear his emotions all over his face—especially when he was thinking lascivious thoughts about Victoria—set her teeth on edge. For his sake, she hoped he proved to be an asset to his team. Otherwise, she was going to end up shoving his face into concrete.

Tegan decided to choose the moment to jog down the dock with a sharp bark. A seabird squawked and took off from the edge of the dock, landing a few feet away on the water. Undeterred, the dog launched off the dock, his long body stretched full length and short legs extended. He hung in the air for a moment in a Superman pose before hitting the water with a splash. The bird took off in a panic of flapping wings. Having successfully defended his territory, Tegan came swimming back up to the shore and climbed out on his own. He waited until he had returned to the group and shook out his fur right next to Jay, sprinkling the man with cold water.

"What kind of dog is he?" It was either ask the question or laugh directly in Jay's face as he cursed at the little dog with the big-dog personality.

Tegan gave her a happy doggie grin.

Roland's eyes sparkled with humor. "Pembroke Welsh corgi."

"Now we've seen the entire exterior, you have any thoughts you want to share?" Adam had kept pace with Victoria as they'd completed not only the first walk around the perimeter, but also the second lap. Tegan had opted to keep them company, which was good because the stocky dog looked to be somewhat chunky despite his earlier antics.

"Mmm." Her gaze swept up and down the walls. "We're going to need to clear a lot of this landscaping, unfortunately. There's too much dead-space."

"Agreed." He had thoughts of his own but he was waiting to add them to hers.

"We're going to want to make a few copies of the property survey and plans of the buildings. I want to mark up several of them and want a set of clean copies too."

"I'll suss it out with Dante before we leave for the evening." Far as he knew, they would be commuting back and forth from Seattle. "You live in downtown?"

"Yes." She was somewhat distracted, still taking images.

"If you don't mind dropping me off back at Safeguard, I'll head back to my flat and upload my pictures. Diaz's second, Scott? She sent me access to the cloud storage secured for our teams." He admired how thorough Victoria was, but she obviously had a chip on her shoulder. She was going back over ground he'd covered, taking images of the same things he had. At first he'd thought she'd caught something he'd missed or wanted different angles. He'd see tonight if her shots were any different from his own.

Could be he could learn something from her. Or he'd know for a fact she was burning energy repeating work already done. It'd be best to talk it out with her early in the project rather than let her go on doing it until she began to resent him.

He took a deep breath and let it out slow. Patience. They were learning to work together. He could build her confidence in him. She seemed reasonable so far. It'd be a better discussion once he had tangible examples to make his point to her.

Of course, if she did decide to butt heads with him on it, at least he enjoyed the glory of her temper. She was beautiful when she'd worked up some anger, and he'd bet her rage was glorious.

"No. Sit." She straightened and stood glowering at Tegan. The tri-colored corgi sat and looked up at her expectantly. "You can't go sniff everything I'm taking a shot of, pup. You're getting into all of my pictures."

Adam grinned. "He's interested in what you're interested in. Sounds like a wise male to me."

She shot him a scathing look over her shoulder before trying to retake her intended image. "Yes, I can drop you back at Safeguard."

He considered her for a few more moments as they wandered across the property to study the main buildings. "Is the ferry closer to your flat than Safeguard is?"

She stopped in her tracks. She chewed her lip, considering. "Yes. Traffic tomorrow morning will be annoying too. People do use the ferry to commute. We'll be going in the opposite direction of the majority of it though."

"Could save you some time if I meet you at your flat." He watched her lips press into a line. Lifting his hands and holding them palms out, he figured he should adjust his offer. "Or I could meet you at a coffee shop nearby. Whatever you'd be comfortable with and still save you the trouble of having to head to Safeguard and double back through downtown to catch the ferry. We're going to be doing this every morning for a while so it makes sense to work out an efficient routine."

"True." Her mouth quirked into the ghost of a smile at his mention of efficiency. The corners of her eyes creased a little with humor. "Yes, it'd be helpful if you met me at a coffee shop. There's one on the street a few yards up from my apartment complex. I'll show you as we head home."

Well, if a man wasn't invited up to a lady's innermost sanctum, her favorite place to acquire caffeine was a close second. He'd take it.

She sighed. "This is going to require more design and strategy than one person can do in the amount of time we have."

He raised an eyebrow at her. "I hope you weren't planning to try on your own."

They were supposed to be partners. He might not have experience working directly with a lady before, but he was confident partnership still meant what he thought it did.

Tucking her smartphone into her jacket pocket, she glanced at Tegan. Then she met Adam's gaze. "I'd planned to take the lead. I'm not so great at delegating. My former partner got to know me well enough to coax tasks out of my hands or beat me to them. It's not exactly fair to expect you to do the same without any kind of warning."

Ah. Well then. Her self-awareness was becoming one of his favorite aspects of her. "You've now warned me. I will do my best to learn to work with you, but we need to agree on this kind of open communication. I can't read your mind to anticipate what you need from me, aye?"

She nodded. "It's going to be a learning exercise for me too. I'll try."

"Do. People like us, we don't try. We do." He glanced at Tegan, still sitting and watching her. "Those ears. They're big for his head, don't you think? All he needs is a robe and a light saber."

Laughing, she headed for the entrance of the main house. "Let's get the tour of the interior of the buildings before we go."

He fell in at her side amicably. "What kind of business issues do you think led to our client needing this level of security?"

"Hmm?" She lifted her shoulder in a one-sided shrug. "I'm still considering the possibilities."

But she wasn't disregarding the risk associated with the cause for all this paranoia. Good. A paranoid person wasn't necessarily wrong. It'd help them protect their client and properly secure his home if they had more context as to how this situation evolved from the beginning.

"Either way, we've got a clear statement of work to guide us." She sounded confident in their organization's document. "Our client might not know what he's leaving out. There's assumptions outlined in the contract to protect us from scope creep."

"Yeah." He drew the affirmative out slowly as he thought on it. "Do you always stick to exactly what's in the contract?"

She slowed a step, and Tegan checked his pace to stay with her. "Not always. I do what there's time to do within the limits of the contract. If we need to put extra effort in to be sure we do the right thing, we will, as long as we've still got the time covered in the contract. The client doesn't always remember what they agreed to in the statement of work."

"They remember that you did the right thing." Or people could end up remembering only the one wrong in a history of solid, good performance. One black mark could erase all the good done in a career.

"Yes. A part of what we're doing here is making

sure our client becomes a positive reference. Safeguard needs a few real wins to counteract some unfounded rumors." She didn't want to share what those might be, he guessed.

"Then we do what needs to be done to make sure our Roland is happy with our work." Adam considered Jay, wondered if he should flag his old friend as a potential risk to the project. Then again, it'd been a couple of years since they'd served together. Adam had changed since then, grown into his skin. All he needed was the chance to prove himself to his new team. The least he could do was give Jay the same opportunity.

"We fulfill the statement of work, every deliverable." She gave him a smile finally. "And to your point, it's not always about what's in the contract or on record. It's about perception of the full experience. We'll make sure Roland has good things to say about his experience with Safeguard."

Adam returned her smile with a grin of his own. "Sounds good, partner."

Chapter Six

Victoria studied the maps of Roland's property again, tapping her pen against her notepad. Laptops were good for the final briefs on her security design and defense strategy, but she preferred the freedom to make notes and scribble on paper in the draft stages. At this point, she'd taken copies of the original plans and marked them up to give her more detailed indications of terrain. Now, she had a clear perspective on low-visibility areas and dead-space.

It'd been a surprise to her when she'd realized the current security team had been limiting their surveillance to the standard perimeter cameras. There'd been several areas of dead-space—places where it was impossible for a person to see while walking the grounds—both on the perimeter and near the main buildings. Some of those spots were gatherings of ornamental shrubs and large bushes in the landscaping. A full-grown person could hide in those in daylight. At night, they were havens of darkness without even lights to keep the areas shadow-free.

She'd made notes for the landscapers to make

changes as soon as possible. If she had to, she'd tear up the shrubs near the house herself.

The property was incredibly vulnerable.

Granted, the current security team had been in place before there'd been a sense of urgency to establish real defense in depth, layers of security and defensive lines designed to defend each other in the case of an attempted incursion. They'd increased the frequency of random patrols of the area in response. What pricked at her was the sudden need for it now. If they had more specifics on why it was suddenly a priority when it so obviously wasn't previously, she'd have a better idea of what she was defending against.

"Partners do not run off and hoard all the work for themselves." Adam sounded seriously irritated.

Victoria resisted the urge to hunch her shoulders. Instead, she forced herself to look up and meet his gaze steadily, even if he was right. "You were completing an important task."

He narrowed his eyes. A muscle twitched in his cheek as he clenched his jaw. "You had me up on the highest part of the main house installing additional surveillance cameras. One of the other bros could've done it just as well."

She shook her head. "They're getting the streaming feed from those, yes. But I wanted you to install them since we're getting the feed from them too."

For those cameras, at least, she wanted a comprehensive view of the property immediately. Eventually, they'd have access to the property's entire surveillance system. This would give them the closest thing to a bird's-eye view in the meantime.

"You're giving me busywork so you can think in peace." He'd spoken with surety and a healthy dollop of frustration.

Placing the pen down, she met his gaze. His intensity slammed into her with almost physical force. "Yes. I think better this way."

"You said yourself this was too much for one person to do alone." His tone had gone flat again and utterly calm.

She was beginning to realize it was not a good sign. He was angry. So far, he tended to be right with his reasoning when he did this.

"This is what I do well." She could start out truthfully. Now that he'd called her out, she wasn't as certain her tactic had been the right thing to do. It'd seemed to make perfect sense when she'd decided the mapping was a priority. "We really did need the increased visuals right away."

His brows drew together. "You don't know what I do well yet. You're not giving me the chance to contribute and that is not fair to our client."

She'd opened her mouth to retort, thinking he'd been about to tell her it wasn't fair. She hadn't expected him to bring their client into it.

"The concept of defense in depth relies on complexity to establish robust protection." His words were measured, logical, and were inexorably reasonable. "When you design the plan on your own, which I'm guessing you've done in the past without someone else calling you out on the way you allot tasks, your plan has a flaw."

It was her turn to clench her jaw. "I am good at what I do."

The corner of his mouth turned up in a grim sort of smile. "Good enough to have been in the business a long while. Tell me, how many professionals out there have gone up against a defense you planned? Have you been keeping count? Can you tell me no one has been studying you over the years? I'm betting somebody, somewhere has gotten inside your head."

Surprised, she remained silent. Thinking. It hadn't happened yet but she preferred not to wait for shit to happen before preparing for the worst.

He snorted, his body posture relaxing a fraction as some of the tension left his shoulders. "It never occurred to you, did it? Humble. You don't give the impression, Queenie. Now we're talking, this isn't even personal, is it? You did this to your previous partner too."

Irritated, she glared at him. "Marc had his skill sets. He liked having hands on the technology setup. He'd look over the plans I developed and provide input after I had the majority drafted."

She wondered now, with Adam's commentary, if Marc had simply figured out how to work with her idiosyncrasies. Working with a wide variety of personalities had been Marc's forte. He'd never complained, but he was possibly the most easygoing man she'd ever met. It was a shocking contrast to Adam's personality.

Her ex's accusations echoed faintly in the back of her mind. He'd always asserted she couldn't compromise to make anything work with anyone. No, she could be flexible. "Do you propose a different way to do this?"

A bit more animation returned to Adam's expression as his eyebrow lifted. "We can brainstorm together over the maps you've got done so far. It'd save time if you don't have to wait for me to review your work and maybe avoid hard feelings later if I have to ask questions where you thought you were clear or if I disagree with you. Let's make this an active collaboration."

He sounded like Kyle, different from Gabe or Lizzy or Marc. Before Safeguard, before Gabe had made the decision to split them into two-man teams, they'd been a part of their parent organization, Centurion Corporation. As Centurions, they were grouped into four- or five-person fire teams. Those fire teams had been grouped into larger squads. Within each fire team, each person had a separate specialty and a different role to play.

She was used to splitting up tasks along the lines of expertise. Marc hadn't had a problem with it because their skills had complemented each other. It literally hadn't occurred to her to apply both hers and Adam's energies to the same task.

"You think it'd be a more effective use of time." She considered it. Every project relied on three major factors: resources, time and budget. If one was a higher priority, they'd need to sacrifice one or both of the others to make it happen. The critical aspect of this project was time. She'd thought to split their resources to manage tasks in parallel, thus saving time. Adam's suggestion could save time in a different way.

"For the planning stage, yes. As we execute tasks later, probably not. We don't know each other well. I'll definitely have questions about your plan. I won't be able to make assumptions. We'd go back and forth a lot to get clarification." He grimaced. Obviously, he didn't enjoy the documentation aspect of working on this sort of project. "We don't have time for the whole draft, review, make changes, review again system. We need to cut out the review time and work on this together."

At least he wasn't suggesting they skip the documentation. Others had tried in the past. It resulted in sloppy work.

"Fine. Pull up a chair." She'd never tried designing strategy in direct collaboration. Come to think of it, she'd been pushed out of such efforts in past lifetimes, before she'd begun her work with the Centurions. "Let's give this a try."

He'd been right about something else too. If the design came only from her, it was a similar approach to other strategies she'd developed in the past. Having him in the mix during the drafting stage was going to add to the complexity of the defense.

He didn't gloat over winning his point. He simply grabbed a chair.

"You've been focusing on vision. I've got a few ideas."

Adam had to give it to Victoria, she was a very detail-oriented individual. It'd been over an hour, and she was still studying the maps with painstaking attention. They had notes on making use of both long-range and short-range cameras. Some of the existing cameras would be repurposed in the new plan as appropriate, but they'd also be installing new technology. A combination of regular visuals, night, heat and infrared capabilities would be put in place. They were even going to train Roland's existing security team on the use of drones.

In addition to the established vision capabilities, there would be layers of precautions. Not every observer would look for more than obvious surveillance. In fact, while some cameras would be left visible, many would be concealed. The idea was for intruders to go for the easy-to-find cameras and disable those, leaving other, less obvious ones intact.

She'd insisted on making note of every detail for the vision aspect of the defense strategy. Their maps now had not only the exact position of every camera but also the range of visibility they would provide in shaded cones. Of course, the cones were color-coded to indicate the capabilities of each camera.

"The surveillance is our best source of intel before and during an incursion." She was pacing, absentmindedly rubbing her lower back.

"Information is key to success." It was a saying somewhere. He was sure of it. Keeping his brain busy tracking down where the phrase came from only partially distracted him from watching her in motion.

She was beautiful. He could get all flowery with the descriptions. But what filled his head wasn't words. It was images and daydreams of touching her again, having her move under his touch in response to the things he wanted to do to her. And he had very good memories of what she could do to him.

Considering how his body was reacting, he remained seated and let the table provide him with some measure of cover. Even in his jeans, she was going to be able to see he was not completely focused on the task at hand. Or maybe she'd assume the concept of defense in depth turned him on.

He'd claim it if she caught him.

"We're almost there." She returned to the table to lean over their maps, one hand bracing a portion of her weight as she leaned past him to snag her pen from the other side of the table. "Once these are complete, we can take a look at setting visible two-man patrols at irregular intervals. We need to harden the target with more intimidating physical presence from the security team."

His cock jumped as she'd mentioned hardening. Hah. Fine. He did find planning arousing when it was her doing the talking.

Her shoulder bumped his, and he placed his hands on the surface of the table in an attempt to keep them off of her. No touching. She had made it clear they were to be a professional partnership.

For now.

"Adam?"

"Yeah." He'd zoned out. Shit.

"Your eyes glazed over." She was studying him, within arm's reach. Her clear gaze was cool, assessing.

She was always measuring the people around her. He wondered if she even realized she did it. The effect was the same as splashing cold water in his face. Being judged did that to a man. "Might be a good time for coffee."

Easing the chokehold he had on his libido, he subtly adjusted himself and stood.

"I'll join you." She reached across the table to sketch another note on one of the maps on the far side.

He groaned, wondering if he dared bite his fist. Because it was either that or reach out and take hold of the very shapely rear she'd presented to him. Being around her sent him back and forth between hot wanting and cold reserve. If he'd wanted to do this to himself, he'd hit a sauna then take a plunge into the bay down at the end of the dock.

She straightened and turned, coming up right against him. Blinking in surprise, she looked up at him through long, dark golden eyelashes. "I thought you'd backed up some."

It would've been the smart thing to do, safer. But his patience had been burned out on work. Now, he was taking a break and riling her up was his newest fun.

"You move fast, Queenie."

She scowled up at him. She wasn't the type to back down or try to the right or left of him either. She could push him though, and he'd give her space. But he wanted her to be direct about it.

Instead, she glared at him. "You need to leave off with the nickname."

"You don't like it?" He cocked his head a little to the side as he studied her.

"It's unprofessional." She blinked a couple of times, and her comment didn't have her usual decisive conviction.

She was carrying a whole lot of baggage. Eventually, it was going to wear her down if she didn't let go of it on her own. Keeping her thoughts to herself likely didn't help at all.

He was curious, in a morbid sort of way, and once in a while he tried to be considerate even if he was being a pain in the ass. "Did your previous partner have a nickname for you?"

He wouldn't tease her with nicknames if someone had tortured her with them in the past.

A shadow crossed her expression. "No. Neither my partner nor my ex did."

"But you don't like them." He was getting lost, quickly, and she was withdrawing into herself.

Her gaze had become unfocused, the spark leaving her eyes. There must be some bad memories tied to the ex. Talking about her former partner didn't do this to her.

She shrugged. "I prefer to carry myself in a professional manner. Impeccable. Respectable. Reliable."

He frowned. As she'd spoken, her comments had cut inward. Far from positive, her words had turned bitter with remembered anger. There was the malaise he'd noticed about her. It'd come and gone throughout their working session. It was a dark, ugly cloud of thought eating her from the inside out. Consuming her and turning her attention deep inside, she wasn't even aware of his proximity anymore.

Well, couldn't have that.

He leaned in and kissed her.

He'd intended to be quick, startle her out of her thoughts. But as soon as their lips met, hers parted in a gasp and he couldn't resist the invitation. He took her deeper, tasting.

She kissed back, drinking him in and leaning into him. Her hands gripped his waist in encouragement.

Just like that, he was on fire and she was living flame under him. He'd backed her up against the table until she was on her back. His hips fit between her legs, grinding until they both groaned with the friction. He gripped her ass until she lifted her legs and wrapped them around his waist. Her hands hooked behind his neck, pulling him in for hungry kisses.

A sharp, happy bark sounded outside.

Sucking in air, he straightened and pulled her up to stand with him. They stumbled back from each other. Each of them dragged their hands through their own hair in an attempt to straighten themselves up.

A minute later, there was a knock on the pool house door.

"Hello? It's Roland. We've lunch up at the main house."

Being drawn to Adam made sense. He was not only charismatic, but a balance of intelligent and creative, practical with a good sense of when it was the right time to take a risk. Incredibly, deliciously gorgeous could be added to her growing list of things she liked about him. He was the whole package, and she was particularly tempted by a man like him. But she'd scratched that itch and she shouldn't be hungry for more.

Obviously, her body didn't agree.

As they all climbed the steps to the front landing leading into the main house, she had the opportunity to appreciate Adam's tight behind. He'd taken the steps two at a time and left Roland to catch up. If anything, their employer had slowed on the steps as Adam passed him. Once Adam reached the landing, he turned and flashed her one of his lopsided grins, sweeping an arm out to take them all in and indicate they should precede him as they went through the front door. Roland paused, cleared his throat and proceeded into his home.

She huffed. Adam was over the top, larger than life, if she was the type of woman to be overwhelmed. But as she entered the main house, having him hold the door for her brought an unaccustomed heat to her cheeks.

She didn't need a man to do anything for her. There was nothing to prove. There'd been plenty of missions over the years when she'd had to establish her worth to a team.

The thing about Adam was the lack of douchebaggery. He didn't doubt her ability or her intelligence. So far, when he questioned her decisions, it was to request she take other options into consideration. If he challenged her, it was as an equal and not with any misguided assumption that he might have the upper hand. He'd simply acknowledged her. Furthermore, he demanded her to be more than she was on her own by utilizing the skills and knowledge he brought to the table.

It'd been a lesson in humility for her, and one she'd needed. It'd pissed her off at first. But she'd cooled down to a sort of wry respect. Man had balls.

He'd spent the last several hours working with her, not in direct conflict with her. It was…nice, the way he made her feel. He'd established his respect for her as a professional and as an independent woman, so it was strange to get the rush out of his small gestures, a pleasant buzz. Sure, she could open a door for herself. It was nice when someone else had the consideration to do it for her. She felt feminine and desired, not because she was a contrast to his masculinity but because she was a match to it.

It was a heady feeling, and she smiled, savoring it.

She shouldn't let it go any further. Her thoughts were already running down paths that were so far beyond the limits of a working relationship, she wasn't going to be able to call them back. Despite today's slip, they would need to go back to cold professionalism. But as he said, they could discuss the chemistry between them after this contract was completed.

In the meantime, he was proving to be a decent partner. So far.

"We generally leave lunch out on the dining room table for people to serve themselves." Roland led them from the foyer, through a sitting area, to the dining room. "Cuisine changes each day so please let me know if you have a preference. I won't promise I'll always accommodate, but I will take your requests into consideration."

Thus far, she and Adam had been working on the grounds security to design layers from the perimeter inward. This gave them the opportunity to consider enhancements to the house without needing a formal tour just yet. She noted the sparse furnishing inside the house first and, in particular, the lack of blinds. Roland was apparently one for fabric curtains. He had separate sets of sheers and heavier drapes. The main house's architecture was elegantly simple in straight lines, echoed in the interior design. The entire house seemed to be an arrangement of rectangular rooms set perpendicular to each other. What furniture there was had a modern look and feel, equally as straightforward in design. In fact, she wasn't sure she could find a single angle in any room that wasn't ninety degrees.

She studied the tops of the window frames. Something was odd about them. "You like a lot of natural light."

"When appropriate, yes." Roland paused near a set of switches on one wall. "But I'm told so many windows can be detrimental to the safety of people inside the house. This house was designed by an eccentric architect with a penchant for reading apocalyptic fiction. I'm told the house could withstand a…zombie apocalypse, if needed."

As he spoke, Roland pressed a button and metal panels lowered on the outside of every window within line of sight. The panels moved slowly, so no one climbing in a window would necessarily be caught and injured, but once they were down, they provided a solid barrier to entry.

"Interesting choice." Adam's voice was rich with

amusement, but he was studying the windows just as closely as she was. She could almost see the gears turning in his head.

The outer security cameras would be that much more important if they decided to make this protected mode of the house an integral part of their defensive plan. They'd need the extra vision.

Tegan trotted past them all, continuing through the living area and around the corner. Well, a dog had different priorities, and he probably knew better than anyone else where there was food to be found.

Victoria glanced up and her gaze locked with Adam's. He'd been looking at her. His smile warmed her from her sternum out to her fingertips and toes. It was not the kind of smile friends or colleagues shared. His carried a different kind of heat.

"Well, then, this will be key as we continue to enhance your security." She tore her gaze away from Adam and tipped her head as she faced Roland.

Their employer removed his glasses and polished them absentmindedly with a soft cloth he'd pulled from his trouser pocket. Then he hit the button to raise the metal shielding, letting natural light back into the house. "I'll try to make a list of any other features to the house that may be of use."

"Excellent."

Roland motioned for them to continue through the room and into the next. It was a good thing too. Victoria was worried her stomach might reach out and consume her from within. Really, she never realized she was hungry until after it was far too late to snack. She was famished.

They turned the corner and walked the length of a bright room furnished with a pair of angular lounge chairs. Despite their obvious purpose, they were still straight lined and very contemporary in style. It was a room for relaxation. On the few sunny days the region had, this room would be flooded with warm sunlight. The windows were floor-to-ceiling here on the outer walls, and a sliding glass door led to a long lap pool. She wondered if it was heated.

Not that there would be time for a swim, of course. But she loved swimming better than any other exercise. Maybe she could arrive early one morning for a swim workout before starting the day, after they'd gotten the majority of the security in place.

They turned again into another room. A huge dining room table was positioned slightly off center in this room, with a buffet along one wall. Set on the buffet was a large selection of black plastic containers with clear lids.

Jay stood leaning against the wall, leaning over the food.

"It's about time you all got here. I'm about starving." His words were delivered in a friendly tone with a slight undercurrent to them.

Victoria slowed. Despite her earlier thoughts, there was no way she was going to hurry to get to the food with him complaining. She'd barely met him and already he irritated her.

"Sorry, bro, we were checking out a feature or two about the house. You probably noticed the shields go down." Adam walked over to the food and stooped low to ruffle Tegan's ears. The small dog sat patiently looking up at the buffet with a hopeful gaze.

"Help yourselves." Roland started opening containers. "But please, don't feed Tegan. He's not allowed 'people' food."

There'd been a slight hesitation and a discomfort in using the term. Maybe he'd picked up the phrase from a veterinarian or the pet supply store. It didn't come naturally from him.

Roland looked down at Tegan. "Go lie down."

The corgi sighed but left the buffet area, skirting around the big dining room table to lie against the opposite wall.

Adam thought he'd had a lot on his mind, but the scent of food rising up from the opened containers set his mouth watering. Damn. Breakfast had been a long time ago.

"I hope you enjoy authentic Chinese cuisine." Roland stood back as Jay grabbed a plate and started to scoop food into his plate with a spoon and fork held together in one fist.

Victoria was still studying the interior, particularly the layout and windows. "We appreciate you providing the meal. We're really not picky."

Depending on the mission or deployment location, food could end up very simple and more designed to provide calories than to taste like…anything. Some bases did a decent job, but they had to cater to mass numbers. During his months in New Zealand, Adam had rediscovered how much good food, made with car-ing hands, could improve a man's life. He wasn't picky either, but he did try to pay attention to good food when he smelled it.

There were quite a few dishes to choose from and most weren't immediately recognizable to him. Didn't matter. He was hungry and his nose promised his mouth a good time. As eager as he was to start, he held back and waited until he caught Victoria's gaze.

He gave her a smile and tilted his head toward the food. She blinked, then took a plate in hand. The faintest hint of pink stained her cheeks. He grinned.

"Where's the General Tso's chicken?" Jay asked around a bite of egg roll, pointing with the remainder of the fried roll toward the buffet.

Adam chuckled. "I'm guessing it's not going to be here."

Roland cleared his throat but didn't confirm.

Jay swallowed and moved around the dining table to sit with his overflowing plate. "Why not? This is Chinese. Every Chinese restaurant has General Tso's chicken. The only thing I recognized over there was stir-fried beef, potstickers, and beef and broccoli."

"There's a few interesting dishes here as well." Victoria hummed happily as she served herself from a dish of greens, shredded pork and bean curd. "And you don't find these pan-fried meat pies on most menus."

"There are pork pies and beef as well." A hint of pleasure colored Roland's voice. "You're familiar with authentic Chinese cuisine, then."

Adam grinned and decided to try a little bit of everything. Sounded like it was going to be one of the best lunches he'd ever had on the job. He even dished up a helping of the stir-fried purple vegetable that was too long and skinny to be the eggplant he was used to seeing in eggplant Parmesan. He froze when Victoria gasped.

"Are these xiao long bao?" She hovered over a container, chopsticks poised.

Roland nodded, making a pleased noise. "They're never as good served this long after steaming, but they're still quite delicious. I heated these again just before coming to ensure they are at least properly hot. If you enjoy all this, perhaps you should visit the restaurant in person once security is complete here."

"These things? Just another kind of dumpling, right?" Jay nabbed one with his fingers.

"They're much hotter inside than you might think. Be careful." Roland even lifted a hand in warning.

Heedless, Jay popped the dumpling in his mouth and bit down. His eyes widened and his lips opened in a large O as he sucked in air and blew it out quickly. Tegan jumped up from his spot on the floor and barked.

Quickly, Victoria grabbed a bottle of water from an ice bucket on the buffet and set it on the table in front of Jay. He tore at the cap and took a long chug of water. "Burned the entire fucking inside of my mouth!"

Adam glanced at the container in question. It was partially covered and steam was still wafting from around the lid.

"Xiao long bao—also called soup dumplings—are my favorite." Victoria turned and began to serve herself a few, unfazed. "Done well, the dumplings have extremely thin wrappers around scalding hot soup and meltingly tender filling. I'm very impressed you've managed to keep them this hot even if you did heat them up before coming to get us. I'm looking forward to trying them before they cool."

Jay growled. "One of those almost killed me and you're still going to eat that?"

"There's a way to eat them without scalding your taste buds into uselessness." Victoria seated herself at the dining room table, several seats down from Jay while still opposite him.

"At your own risk." He scowled and applied himself to the mound of stir-fried beef on his plate. Adam shook his head. Jay must've fished for the beef, leaving behind the broccoli in the dish.

Sitting directly across from Victoria, Adam waited for Roland to serve himself and join them. Tegan resumed his sad spot on the floor against the wall. Almost as one, they started eating. Adam went for the beef pie first. He'd never had something like the pan-fried round pastry. It was crispy on the outside though the pastry was moist and soft on the inside, and the filling was savory, seasoned beef.

Focused as he was on the food, he watched Victoria place one of her soup dumplings on her spoon and poke it precisely with her chopsticks. As steaming hot broth spilled out, she sipped at her spoon and closed her eyes. Pleasure suffused her expression, her lashes casting delicate shadows on her cheeks. Then her lashes lifted as she looked down at her dumpling and placed a few shreds of ginger marinated in some sauce on it. She finally ate her dumpling off the spoon.

"Oh." She chewed slowly and swallowed. "Those are quite nice."

"Mmm." Mouth too full for words, Roland's tone and nod indicated his agreement. It took him a few chews and a swallow before he could form words. "Normally, I wouldn't bother to have xiao long bao as takeout. I'd only order good ones at the restaurant when I have time to enjoy them immediately when served. But these are good enough to be worth bringing home cooled."

"You call that cold?" Jay was still in a surly mood as he continued to eat. "You said you heated them up again. Nothing needs to be that hot. What the fuck?"

There was a pause as everyone at the table fell silent.

"Of course, the reheating helps, but the best flavor is immediately on serving." Roland's posture was stiff as the man continued to eat.

Great. The last thing they wanted to do was piss off the man who held their contract.

Glaring at Jay, Adam took a sip of his own water. "Generally, people are friendlier once they've had a mean as feed like this."

"A what?" Jay's brows came together in a deeper scowl. "You saying I'm mean?"

"Nah, bro." Adam held up his hands, empty. "I'm saying we all are usually better people with full bellies. There's a lot of good food here."

Jay stared at him for a long moment, then shrugged, his face clearing. "Yeah. It's all right. I don't know what kind of place this is if they don't have General Tso's chicken though. Can't be legit."

"I'll keep that in mind." Roland sounded amiable, but there was an undertone of brittle irritation.

Victoria raised an eyebrow, then met Adam's gaze. Adam decided to apply himself to his plate so he could get seconds. Last time he'd checked, General Tso's chicken wasn't particularly considered a measure of any restaurant's level of authenticity. He'd thought the dish was an American thing evolved from Chinese cooking. Thanks to Jay, this might be the last time their employer treated them to this particular lunch again.

Ah, Jay, the ass never learned. It'd been a few years now, but he was still rude as hell. It might be a good idea to share some of Adam's personal experience working with Jay when he and Victoria went over the personnel files this evening. Design and implementation were in their scope as part of the Safeguard contract. Jay was part of the in-house security team. But in order to secure the multilayer security system they were deciding, the on-site security needed to be flawless and on point twenty-four hours a day.

The trick would be finding the right time and striking the right balance of sharing background information, without personal bias.

There were a lot of things Adam would rather forget about his last deployment with the US military, but he chose to remember exactly how hit-and-miss Jay's performance had been in the past. The other man could've changed. The couple of years had changed Adam. But looking at Jay now, Adam was doubting any changes had been for the better.

Chapter Eight

The streets of Seattle were quiet with an hour or so yet to dawn. Streetlights still held shadows back until the rising sun could arrive to cast light even through the usual cloud cover. Little to no traffic was going to be a good thing for them, but the real challenge to getting back to their client quickly was going to be the ferry.

Adam didn't wait for Victoria to bring her vehicle to a stop before grabbing for the door handle and hopping into the passenger seat. For her part, she barely waited for him to close the door before pulling back onto the street. They were going to be first in line to board the ferry, no doubts about that.

"Unmanned alarm was triggered ten minutes ago. On-site security acknowledged the alarm one minute after trigger. Local authorities just arrived. Security team is coordinating with local authorities to clear the property." He made the report as he settled his ass into the seat and pulled the seat belt across his torso. He placed his backpack in the seat well, between his feet.

It was going to be a rough wait for the ferry to make it across the Sound.

"Too long." Victoria's words came out clipped. There was no censure in her tone, only a grim statement of fact. "It's taking us too long to get there."

"Agreed." He wasn't exactly chipper either. Neither of them needed coffee though, not with adrenaline zinging through both of them after the alarms had gone off back at their client's property.

Based on the initial briefing, there'd been nothing to indicate an immediate threat. There was no clause in the contract specifying response time from the Safeguard team. Sure, Roland had seemed jumpy, but even their client hadn't indicated he expected the new security measures to be tested right away. He'd simply wanted the redesign to progress as quickly as possible. It'd seemed as if there was time to prepare for impending issues.

But when the alarm had been triggered, both Adam and Victoria had received notifications. Then she'd texted him to let him know she was en route and to be ready. He'd already been rolling out of bed and rolling extra pieces of clothing to stuff into his pack. It went unsaid: the spirit of their contract was to keep their client safe, which meant they needed to get there. Posthaste.

He pulled his laptop out of his backpack. "Quick scan of the visual feed from the time of the alarm shows no trespassers. The AI software picked up something, but it's not anything to be seen with the human eye. Not on night vision, not infrared, not CCTV."

The system already in place on Roland's property before they'd started the upgrades had only had closed-circuit television. Adam and Victoria had added the rest.

"Visuals were the first update we made. What else could've triggered the system? Can't you isolate?" There was a thread of irritation in her voice now.

Or maybe he was reading too far into his new partner's tone. A thousand muttering words rose up in his memory. Sure, no one ever said exactly what they had thought to his face years ago. He'd been debriefed in private. What'd been discussed during his debrief had been confidential. The actual truth of his last mission buried under so much…whatever. That'd been a long time ago. He'd made his peace with his decisions, and he was still convinced it'd been the right thing to do even if it had been a dead end to his military career. He'd been given an honorable discharge at least.

This was a different situation. Safeguard, and Victoria, were giving him a new chance. Clean slate. There was no need to trip himself up with worrying about the past. He needed to focus on the here and now.

Victoria hadn't voiced judgment. She'd asked for information. It was on him to provide the answers, fast.

"AI registered line of sight broken between multiple points simultaneously. I need to take a look at the feed directly to see what might've constituted a break in line of sight." He scowled as she came to a hard stop at the line for the ferry. "But the chances of several points, at the same time, indicates an issue with the software to me. I'll check both but looking into the software is going to take longer."

Victoria sighed. "I can't help until we board the ferry, but then maybe we can divide and conquer. I can look at the visual feed while you dive into the software."

She paused, and the air was heavy with unspoken thoughts. His temper rose but he grappled with it. "Best clear the air while we're still on our way there. If you've got tough questions to ask, ask them now."

"Is it possible this was a mistake in install of the software?" Her voice was steady. "We don't tend to use software prone to bugs."

He held his breath for a count of five, then let it out slow. He wanted to defend himself, be angry that she didn't have faith in his abilities. But the reality was that she didn't know him well yet. This was their first mission, first time working together. If they were going to be partners when they arrived back at the property, he needed to build more of the trust between them now. Which meant he had to keep his mind wide open. Even if he knew he'd done everything right, he had to recognize her confidence in him wasn't instantaneously there. It would build over time. If she didn't have it, perception would matter more than reality and the rest of this mission would be a clusterfuck.

"True. This software is cleared by Safeguard and Centurion Corporation. It's not so new that it'd have a lot of bugs to work out." He made himself nod as he acknowledged her point. "But let's keep in mind that every new release of even stable, established software can end up with regression bugs. That's why software releases have hot fixes. Either install issue or software bug are still fair possibilities. I'm going to have to take a closer look to answer your question but I am careful when I set up my software in a system."

She nodded. "Is it possible to have that answer before we get there?"

Heat seared his ears and forehead, and he fought to keep his own tone reasonable. "What are you going to tell the client if I did fuck up the install?"

Getting thrown under the bus was nothing new to him. Hell, he'd just been trying to leave the raw memories of having been made into a scapegoat behind him. This line of discussion was starting to feel very familiar, and he didn't want to sit around for it.

But he had to. He couldn't run from his reputation forever. Obviously, time wasn't going to make it disappear either. Safeguard was taking a chance with him, and if he walked away at the first sign of doubt in him, then he hadn't earned their trust anyway.

It stuck in his throat to sit there and wait for Victoria's answer instead of throwing the car door open and walking away, but he stayed put. Had to. He had something to prove to Safeguard and to his new partner.

Victoria had been watching him for the last few seconds, her clear blue gaze taking in his posture and expression. He probably looked stubborn as hell at the moment. "If it was a mistake, we take ownership and fix it."

She'd said "we." Too simple. Much as he'd have liked for them to be that cohesive a team, it was still too new for them. "That so?"

"Then we need to adjust the way we work." Her gaze remained steady, locked with his. "I will want to quality-check everything you do after this, until we build up a working level of reliability."

He barked out a laugh and it sounded harsh even to his ears.

Her expression darkened and her brows drew together. "You don't think that's fair?"

He rolled his shoulders, trying to ease the tension and relax his posture. He needed to de-escalate this discussion. It was mostly his fault it'd gotten here. "It's fair. More than fair. It's...not something I'm used to."

He hadn't meant to let the last bit out but, hell, she could make of it what she pleased.

"Look, everyone has history." He considered how to give her enough information to understand his reaction. He wasn't ready to take a deep dive into ancient history, not yet. "It's been my experience that a mistake is like a hot potato. It doesn't matter who made it, no one wants to take accountability for it and whoever does ends up burned."

She nodded, focusing front as she drove the car onto the ferry.

"I'm surprised." He dug for words but he was obviously coming up short. "Surprised you're willing to keep me on this mission and work up to being able to trust me again. It sounded like crap for me to laugh like that, but there it is. I should be more grateful."

Victoria huffed. "To be fair, I didn't trust you that far yet anyway. It's been pointed out to me fairly recently that I don't trust anyone to do anything right. My need to check up on people borders on obsessive—or so I'm told. So whether this turns out to be your mistake or the software, I'll be up front and admit I'm probably going to double-check both of our work anyway."

So much wry bitterness in her tone. Someone had ripped her up using a lot of words, twisting them so they sounded accurate when they were meant to do her serious damage. He found his defensive anger turning in a different direction. Whoever had hurt her should suffer an agonizing sort of misfortune.

When she put the car in park, safely on the ferry, he waited until she turned to look at him again. Deliberately, he released his seat belt and turned in his seat to face her. "If you're going to double-check everything, Queenie, feel free to check me over inch by inch while you're at it. I don't mind."

She froze, and for a second he thought she might blow up in his face. Instead, she threw her head back and laughed.

"You are incorrigible." She gasped the statement out between breaths. "Hand me my pack from the back seat, and let's get to checking the data we have before I get completely distracted."

He complied with a grin. Victoria Ash might not realize what she'd admitted but he wouldn't forget. He planned to distract her even more at the first appropriate opportunity he could find, or inappropriate moment if he couldn't wait that long.

"Where have you been?" Roland rushed forward to meet them as they cleared the front entrance to the main house.

Victoria paused, waiting for Adam to step inside and join her. He'd been defensive in the car, but he'd pushed through his initial reaction and gotten to work. If he'd done anything else, she'd have tossed him off the ferry into the Sound. Instead, a growing respect was building, and she didn't want to think too hard about how much it added to her estimation of him. Not yet.

The time stuck on the ferry had been productive, and they'd been able to rule out several possible causes for the alarm trigger.

Which was both good news and bad news. Considering the wild look in Roland's wide eyes, their client was not going to take the bad news with anything resembling calm.

"We came as soon as the alarms were triggered." She tried for soothing but stopped as Roland's jaw tightened. Ah hell, her ex used to say her version of calm was about as comforting as holding on to an iceberg neck deep in freezing ocean. Apparently her ex had been right.

"We're here now." Adam held up his hands, palms outward, drawing Roland's still panicked gaze. "We've checked in with your security team and received a quick debrief. Both Victoria and I analyzed the data from the security feeds on the way over so we've not wasted any time."

"So what set off the alarms?" Roland backed away from the edge of panic visibly.

She didn't blame their client. Adam's voice had an almost hypnotic quality to it. She found herself drawn in every bit as much as Roland was.

"We can tell you no one set foot on the property." Adam gave Roland the good news first. "Every one of the visual feeds confirms there were no trespassers, and your security team on-site has already cleared the grounds. They're conducting a second check now, not just to confirm the grounds are clear but to double-check for any signs of someone who might have come and gone. Nothing so far."

"Okay." The vein pulsing at Roland's temple slowly disappeared.

Good. It would've been very bad if they'd had to call an ambulance. The man had been a few minutes away from giving himself a stroke.

"We can also tell you the artificial-intelligence software installed for detection was installed correctly." She tried her best to imitate the warmer tone Adam used and was rewarded by a slight uptick at the corner of Adam's mouth. Fine. He could be amused. "We're going to stay and continue to analyze the data until we track down exactly what triggered the alarms."

Roland nodded, the motion jerky as he tried to swallow at the same time. "Stay. Yes. Excellent. I should've insisted on it anyway. You two being across the way in Seattle is too far. I want you to stay on the premises until the security system is fully in place."

Victoria opened her mouth to argue and then thought better of it. Adam was waiting for her answer.

The level of fear and anxiety coming off of Roland in waves didn't match the behavior of someone worried about a simple incursion of privacy. The man was beyond afraid for his life.

Staring at him, she waited until he met her gaze directly. There was a pleading in his expression she hadn't seen previously. The man was desperately afraid, and he was hiding something behind that fear.

"Are we here to secure your property?" She asked the question quietly, making sure the words would only be heard by the three of them even if someone else or some sort of listening devices were present in the house. "Or are we here to keep you alive?"

Adam stilled next to her but didn't project any surprise. He was a smart man. She'd no doubts of that even if she wasn't sure about a great many things when it came to him. No. She was certain he was waiting for Roland's response, like her.

Roland's eyes widened until the whites showed, and his throat worked as he swallowed hard again. One long second passed and another. A long shudder ran through the man, and he pulled himself together with obvious effort. "I thought if you could secure my property, this house would be safe."

Victoria listened carefully to his words. Considered. "There is a difference."

After another pause, Roland calmed further. "Stay. Please. My life is in this place. Make it safe. I'll call your headquarters in the morning and arrange for whatever addendum to the contract is necessary for bodyguard services."

"You didn't answer the question." Another contractor might've taken her client at his word. She cared more about what had gone unspoken.

"I've already agreed to add to your contract," Roland snapped. His eyes darted to the left and right, his gaze landing on anything around them but her and Adam.

He still hadn't given them everything they needed to know. The man had too many secrets, and they were getting in the way of their ability to protect him. As much as she hated to delve into his privacy, he needed to give them full disclosure to do their job right.

"It's also important for us to have the right assumptions in place." She made sure her tone remained neutral despite the escalation in tension. "How we provide your security changes if it's a difference between protecting a structure or protecting a life."

Roland was silent, his face purpling with frustration and intense emotion. After a long moment, he let air rush out through his clenched jaw. "Every life in this household is to be protected. Mine, Tegan's. Every. Life. Does that answer your question sufficiently, Miss Ash?"

Push the man any further and he'd have a stroke. She gave him a nod, not risking any further verbal sparring. She'd gotten the nuance she needed to adjust their security design appropriately, at least for now.

Chapter Nine

Victoria pressed her hands flat on the desk to either side of her laptop. "My entire morning has been a waste."

"Hardly." Adam lifted his arms, placing his hands behind his head and arching back in his chair for a joint-popping stretch. "We've gone through every aspect of the security on the local network and the monitoring systems twice over. That's a massive undertaking to finish in a day."

"Obviously, we missed something." She kept her gaze fastened to her laptop monitor, ignoring his physical activity with every stubborn fiber in her. Stretching all those delicious muscles was a horribly effective distraction neither of them could afford at the moment. Really. "It's likely to be some setting conflict, and we can't close out system testing with this kind of issue recurring."

As it was, Roland had fretted himself into exhaustion when the alarm had gone off before dawn. He'd accepted the information they'd known when they'd arrived, but he'd be expecting more answers once he woke.

To Adam's credit, he hadn't even blinked when she'd

insisted they go through every aspect of the data and the system logs again. He'd worked with her all day with a matching focus. Even her former partner, Marc, would've taken a break to get lunch.

"It's not a configuration mistake." His words came out clipped, bringing her out of her thoughts. He was so laid-back, the hint of temper actually made her look up from her screen to see him sitting straight in his chair, his spine stiff with tension. "I know my work, and we've checked it over once and again. I've gone along with this thus far, but we're going to need to start considering other causes before we're faced with a situation we're not prepared for because we spent too much time hunting for what isn't there."

She sighed. "What else could it be?"

She'd expected him to scowl or give one of his saucy grins and say something witty. Instead, he studied her with a neutral expression. His gaze was steady, somber. "We're looking for a mistake. There was no one on the property, nothing, not even a stray cat or squirrel. Because there was no incursion, we're assuming there was something wrong with the system. I say we're asses."

"You're not making sense." She came to her feet though, restless. Something. Something wasn't right. He had a point there. A feeling of being blind and stupid had been riding her all day, and it wasn't because of anything he'd said or done.

"This mission hasn't been what we'd expected from the start." Adam stood as well, but he simply moved to snag a dry-erase marker in the study they'd appropriated to do their work. Sparingly furnished with sleek desk surfaces and ergonomically optimal chairs, the walls were painted in bright colors with the kind of paint that allowed the entire wall surface to be used with dry-erase markers. The room had been designed to be a think tank, and they'd decided to make use of it. "Security was the key objective in the original contract."

As he spoke, Adam reached up and wrote the word on the wall, beginning a mind map. The long-sleeved shirt he wore was close-fitted, the soft fabric clinging to him like second skin. His muscle rippled across his back as he wrote.

"But there's different kinds of security, and it's not privacy Roland wants, it's safety." More words went up on the wall. "Let's start thinking about who he wants to be safe from instead. He's not worried about paparazzi the way celebrities would be."

She decided to go along with his mind map. He was thinking in a different direction than she'd been and it wasn't a bad thing.

"No. He was afraid this morning. People can get irritated or angry about invasions of privacy, but they're not afraid the way he was." She considered the sweaty, disheveled appearance. Roland had leaped out of his bed when the alarm had gone off and freaked out inside his own house waiting for them to arrive. He hadn't gone out to his security team.

Adam wrote the word *fear*. "People are afraid when their well-being is threatened. Stalkers. Death threats. He didn't say he'd received those."

"Safeguard would've asked when scoping the contract." She made herself a note to ask Gabe more about both the initial talks and this morning's addendum. Gabe was better at reading people than she was. She didn't connect with clients well.

"The security team didn't mention any either. Dante, at least, would've been aware of any." Adam wrote the word *threat* on the wall with question marks. "So there is a threat, but we don't know what it is, other than life-threatening. And we don't know how Roland knows there is a threat."

She stared at the words on the wall. "If we believe him and don't consider him delusional, then there is an external threat. Immediate and serious."

"Jay thinks Roland is delusional." Adam's voice turned grim. "Ray and Brian just plan to do their jobs well, regardless. So to them, it doesn't matter."

"It should." She drew her brows together, continuing to look at the words *fear* and *threat*. "It's not just about doing what you're paid to do. What do you think about Jay's assessment? You've worked with him in the past, right? How good is he at judging these things?"

"I meant to talk to you about him earlier, but there were other priorities." Adam shook his head. "My experience with the man could be biased, and not in a good way."

Victoria raised her eyebrows. "He seemed friendly toward you."

"Yeah nah. He's that way to anyone he comes into contact with, really. Problem with him, you can't tell if he's on your side ever. He always seems to be but you're always left wondering. To be fair, I could be bitter. I'm not overly fond of anyone from my last unit." Adam paused, then scratched his jaw. "I've never seen him make particularly good use of his people skills. I don't think he'd be sensitive to Roland's concerns. He's more likely to cast his employer in a negative light on principle. He's the type to resent the hand that feeds him, if you know what I mean."

"Ah." Victoria considered. She could see it in Jay. He had a way of staring after the other men around him, seething. If something was done well by anyone else, he made it out to be less of an achievement than it was. Small, petty, and a tendency she would mark as someone not to work with voluntarily in the future.

Adam stepped back, drawing her attention to him and tapping the dry-erase marker against the palm of one hand. "If one of us was planning an attack on this place, what would we do?"

Easy. Planning an attack was easier in her mind than planning the defense of a place. She immediately ran through any number of possible approaches to gather information about the defenses and security.

And his point hit her right in the chest. "The alarm. It wasn't to check to see if there was an alarm. It was to time the response from the security team and local police."

Possibly, it was to time how long it would take for Victoria and Adam to arrive on site.

Adam turned to face her. "There is an impending attack in the works. We have no idea what the scale is or even why. But Roland is not delusional."

Suddenly, this mission was a whole lot more serious, and Adam, to her eyes, was looking incredibly dangerous.

"Let's get back to setting up the layered defenses then." Before she jumped him, right against the wall.

* * *

Adam opened both doors of the refrigerator and stared at the contents with a sigh. Decently stocked with vegetables, he didn't see a single treat or piece of junk food anywhere. There was no sign of Chinese or any of the lunches from the earlier days in the week either. There was no beer, no soda. Roland ate healthy and apparently had a thing about disposing of leftovers.

A whine caught Adam's attention, and he looked down to find Tegan sitting at his feet. The corgi was quiet, unexpected on the stone tiles of the kitchen.

"Sorry, bro, Roland says the house rules are no treats for puppies."

Big brown eyes stared up at him. Adam looked away. He'd withstood the pleading of grown men and children, women even, but somehow a dog had him taking another look in the refrigerator for some sign of something tasty. Maybe it was because Tegan at least was a genuine soul around the place.

Roland was hiding things. Hard to protect a man who didn't tell them what they were supposed to keep him safe from in the first place. The men on the security detail weren't particularly suspicious, but everyone had something in their past. Skeletons, ghosts, mistakes. Victoria was online with the Safeguard databases running deeper background checks on all of the security team members, including Jay. Adam had some insight on Jay's past military experience, but he'd add those details to whatever files Victoria pulled up. But Adam's gut told him whatever was going on wouldn't be as simple as a background search to turn up their threat.

Victoria had issues haunting her too. She wasn't

sharing, and he'd have been surprised if she had. In the short time he'd known her, he got the impression she was more a person of action than a person for sitting down and baring one's deepest, darkest thoughts. Even to herself.

"You have a good life," he told the dog. It was a simple life. Live, eat and care about the people in the household. Maybe love his master.

Adam had long since noticed not every pet loved its master. Oh, they were capable of unconditional love, but pets didn't always bond that way with their owners. An owner could buy all the toys and pet beds and food in the world, but a pet gave its love on its own.

From what Adam had observed, Tegan liked Roland plenty. But the dog's jovial attitude was about the same with Roland as he was with Adam or Victoria or even Dante. Tegan didn't shower Roland with affection and definitely didn't keep track of where Roland was every moment of the day. Take now, for example. Tegan was in the kitchen with Adam, not lying outside Roland's room.

A dog in love with his master would not only know where his master was every minute of the day, but would do his best to have a clear line of sight on his master at all times.

That, to Adam, was just one of many things that were off about this household and this mission. Too many puzzle pieces seemed to be missing. He and Victoria couldn't get a good picture of the situation.

Tegan let out a sort of groaning growl and flipped onto his back, paws waving in the air. Adam looked down at the dog's long torso and comparatively short legs. "You are ridiculous. I can see why you don't get treats. You're heavy for such a short dog."

Heavy was bad for dogs and people. Too much weight was rough on the joints. Even if he'd found something for the dog, Adam would've respected Roland's rules about feeding Tegan for the dog's own health. It was amazing how chubby the corgi was.

"C'mon, dog. Let's sit and drink water. It's probably the only thing in here we want and need at the same time." There was plenty of health food in there, but Adam rarely wanted veggies in their raw form. There'd been times in his deployments when he'd been tempted to kill for a sip of clean water.

Tegan got to his feet readily enough and followed Adam. Adam poured some water from a water bottle into Tegan's bowl and then slid down the wall to sit beside it. The dog lapped up some water, then proceeded to sit on Adam's foot. He was a really genial canine.

"You're trusting me not to boot you across the room. You sure about that?"

The corgi twisted to look up at him and panted at him with a doggie grin, butt firmly planted on his shoe.

"Well, fine. Trust me. But you know, people take trust for granted. They meet people with a sense of entitlement, expecting strangers to trust them. More people give a basic level of trust to absolute strangers than respect." Adam sighed and leaned his head back against the wall. "We trust people immediately, at least so far. Then if you burn us, we make people earn our trust a second time. But the damage is done, trust is a hundred times harder to earn after it's gone the first time.

Probably doesn't make sense. But it's damned easy to undermine trust anyway, so I guess it doesn't matter."

Tegan sighed and lay down, his torso warming Adam's foot.

"All it takes is some gossip, a whispered word or two. Suddenly people are giving you the side eye. You know, the things I had to learn when I first started working with people weren't about trusting my teammates. It was about managing perception so my team would trust me. It's not about truth or what's reality. It's about perception, what people think of you."

Adam took a sip of his water and wished it were beer, maybe something stronger. Victoria seemed to have a thing for scotch. "Now, Victoria, she doesn't give much trust. I like that about her."

They'd been good together. Really good. Scorching hot and fun. But she hadn't stayed with him, even though he'd extended the invitation. It hadn't bothered him either. He'd guessed she wouldn't be able to sleep with a man she'd only recently met, even if she'd had much more carnal relations with him. Victoria had a pure quality about her. She wasn't heartwarming or snuggly. But she was genuine. With her, there hadn't been any pretense, only mutual enjoyment.

Her perception of him mattered. Safeguard's perception mattered too, but from a more objective perspective.

He was certain he was on the right track with his brainstorming. Once they'd continued to consider the issues with the triggered alarm from the angle of a real external threat, the alarm made more and more sense.

What he hadn't discussed with Victoria was the relief he'd experienced when she'd followed his lead. A knot in his chest had eased when their investigation had no longer been about proving or disproving whether the mistake had been his. He was confident he hadn't made a mistake. But it had been a slow, twisting knife the entire time they searched for a cause.

Even now, he was in the kitchen on his own. She hadn't followed him. It spoke of several levels of trust. She wasn't keeping an eye on him, for one thing. Or at least when her gaze was on him, it wasn't out of suspicion.

He grinned at that.

For another thing, she trusted him to take a reasonable break and come back to rejoin the work. She hadn't felt the need to admonish him to come back quickly. And as far as he could tell, they'd gotten past her initial tactic of sending him off elsewhere so she could do the real work by herself.

All good things as far as he was concerned.

He wanted to know more about Victoria. Curiosity drove him to figure out what made her tick and what he could do to surprise her into unguarded expressions. He liked watching her take pride in her work and gain satisfaction from a job well done. She was adorable when she was caught up in solving some difficult issue, and she was truly impressive when angry.

She had a range of emotions and he wanted to explore them all.

In order to pursue that, he had to gain more of her trust. In return, he found himself wanting to give her more of himself too.

And it'd been a long time since he'd been tempted that way.

Chapter Ten

Victoria stood and paced the length of the study, eyeing the wall with their scribbled notes. They'd need to erase it soon. It would be better for the thoughts of fear and threat to remain between her and Adam. They had a better idea of what they were up against.

If they had opponents here on the property, those opponents didn't need to know what she and Adam were thinking.

She'd tried to refute their suspicions from a variety of approaches. Despite having checked the installation and video feeds on the ferry this morning, she'd gone over them again. Had to. She needed to have absolute confidence they hadn't overlooked something. She needed to know she hadn't missed something.

For his part, Adam had taken it with grace. Having your work checked over was never easy. She hated it, personally, but recognized the necessity. He'd been tense but aside from his initial defensiveness in the car, he'd been taking it with much better aplomb than anyone she'd ever partnered previously. And he could've made it harder for her, less comfortable. Instead, he'd constructively applied himself to other work and then taken himself off to the kitchen for a break.

Honestly, she couldn't say she'd have handled it better.

Here she was, finished yet another check and having to stare at the wall again. There was something seriously wrong with the assumptions they'd had going into this project, and it didn't bode well for their success. In her experience, and she had years of it in any number of dangerous situations, the best outcomes arose from missions with the proper scoping and planning at the outset. Every good team had the flexibility to meet changes on the fly head-on and adapt their plan to fit. But it was a grim truth that the measure of success changed along with the other variable on the mission. It didn't take much for mission objectives to go from clearly defined goals to simple survival.

Here, on domestic soil, it was harder to imagine the worst-case scenario. But if she didn't, and Adam's expression as he'd written on this wall told her he had considered it too, then they were likely to lose lives. The fear in Roland's eyes had been real. A threat did exist. If they underestimated it, their client or his security team or they could pay the price.

Whatever this was, it was the opening move of an unseen player. She didn't like it one bit.

"Hydration is a good thing, I hear." Adam entered the study, Tegan trundling close at his heels on short legs. His claws must be well-trimmed because she didn't hear him at all now and had only ever heard him on the tile floor when he was in a rush to get somewhere. Come to think of it, Roland walked quietly as well. Victoria wondered how the man had developed the habit. Most people tended to move comfortably through their own home. Footsteps, random knocks and bangs happened all the time as people picked things up or set them down on various surfaces. Since Roland had retired to his room to rest and leave them to their work, she hadn't heard him.

Odd.

Adam wiggled the water bottle in front of her. "Think hard, drink water too."

She shot him a quick glare and took the water bottle. "Thank you."

He turned to assess the wall and his words. "Thinking on these things."

"Yes, and taking them a step further." She rose and took the dry-erase marker in hand. She wrote the word *quiet* and explained her line of thought to Adam.

He nodded. "You're right. He's not trained silent. You can hear him moving around from the kitchen. But the man definitely doesn't make much sound for a civilian. Could be he's scared, but I think he has some practice staying hush."

She pressed her lips together. "How long has he been afraid? How long has he been hiding inside his own space?"

The contract negotiation had gone quickly. It hadn't been much time for someone to develop mannerisms like the ones they were observing in their client.

"While it's good to take note, I'm not sure how long is immediately important to know." Adam made the suggestion carefully. "We've got resources who can research that off-site. With us here, now, our time might be better spent taking active steps."

She turned away from the board and stared at him. "Understanding the situation is foundational to deciding the next step."

He held up his hands. "Identifying what happened and figuring out why was important. I agree. We did that. After this latest check, what conclusions did you come to?"

His expression was open, earnest. He was trying to work with her. She deliberately relaxed her jaw. She could try to do the same in return. "Install was done correctly. Looking over the visual feeds, I came to the same conclusions we did on the ferry. Everything is working correctly but there was nothing to trigger the alarm. Best I can tell, someone is testing the alarm for other reasons like we said."

Adam nodded. "So what can we do to counter someone gathering intel on our security?"

She held up a hand. "Before we go down that rabbit hole, I want to get something out first."

Expression drained from Adam's face, his animated expressions stilling to a neutral mask. "Yes?"

This was his way of bracing. He didn't know what she was going to say next, and he was protecting himself. Maybe protecting her from his reaction too. She wondered at the intensity of emotion this man experienced if he'd learned to bottle it all up so effectively. It must cost him so much to do it.

"I'm sorry."

He blinked. "You don't need—"

She met his surprised gaze directly. "I do. You've been doing everything you can to work with me. You've accommodated all my working idiosyncrasies and respected what I needed to do in order to make sure we proceeded based on what I thought was necessary. I've made you re-check your work, and I've personally checked your work not once but twice. Anyone else would've been insulted. It is an insult, in a way, regardless of the situation. So, I'm sorry."

It'd been eating away at her this entire morning. She'd had good reasons for her actions and she still firmly believed she'd done the right things. However, maybe her past relationships with her ex and with her last partner had taught her a few things. She was sick of parting ways all torn up. Her divorce was leaving her in shreds and it wasn't quite over yet. The hollowness of Marc's decision to leave the private security business didn't sit with her much better. This working relationship—plus more—building with Adam was different from either of those experiences. At the very least, she didn't want to say goodbye to him feeling the way she had.

It meant trying to make it different, now, in the middle of whatever this was between them.

He didn't drop her gaze, but he stood there with his weight forward on the balls of his toes and the tension in his shoulders ready to fight. After a long moment, his shoulders relaxed. "Apology accepted."

All right. She relaxed too. A huge weight had lifted from her chest, and knots in her belly relaxed. She hated apologies. But it was for the best, because she wanted to move forward with him as her partner and he deserved the consideration.

It wasn't something she'd done well in the past.

"Let's consider next steps, then." Adam wiped the

wall clean. "Where are we going to work from here on out? Out in the guesthouse, or here in the main building? Whichever one it is, we're going to need to secure it for just us."

Adam put a little more strength into wiping the dry-erase surface clean than might have been strictly necessary. For one thing, he didn't want to leave the words remotely visible in even a residual ghost appearance on the wall. For another, he wanted to give Victoria a moment to regain her composure. In the moments of her apology to him, he'd seen her very exposed.

Someone had hurt her, recently. It stoked a deep burning anger inside him. In their business, confidence was a must, bordering on infallible arrogance. They needed to believe in themselves to a point where success wasn't a logical percentage, but instead a visceral foregone conclusion. Any shadow of doubt meant failure. So they left no room for it within themselves.

It took a distinct strength to open oneself up and apologize.

Every day he worked alongside her, he was finding Victoria to be the singular, most complex, powerful personality and heart he'd had the honor to meet. And he was equally certain she'd rip him to shreds for telling her so. Not because it wasn't true or because she wouldn't believe his statement, but because saying the words would crumble her outer defenses. She'd erected the metaphorical equivalent of a great wall around herself. It was impervious to insult, to doubt, to any of the damage a generally misogynistic world could hurl in her direction. She wasn't equipped to handle sincere admiration.

Which meant she hadn't been accorded it nearly enough in her life.

Victoria cleared her throat. "So we have someone, individual or a group, intent on breaking our security and getting to our client. They tested our outermost perimeter alarm and response time early this morning. What steps can we take to render their data useless?"

Adam turned, a grin tugging at the corners of his mouth. He very much enjoyed the way she recovered and got back to business. Her mind worked fast, and in his opinion, it was extremely sexy. "This morning, they timed the response of the on-site security and the local police. They also timed us coming over from Seattle. We're staying on-site now."

She nodded, sitting at the desk and beginning to type on her laptop. "Speaking of which, I'm going to ping Safeguard and have someone swing by my flat to pick up some supplemental clothing and additional gear. Lizzy will do it for me."

"Good call." The grin slipped away. She'd been a part of Safeguard much longer than he had. There was no one he'd trusted with the keys to his own flat.

Blue eyes stared at him, and her gaze held a knowing with a touch of warmth. "What are your sizes? Lizzy can make sure to pick up a few extra pairs of undergarments and shirts while she's making the run. Plus some extra ammunition for the gear you have with you."

She hadn't asked if someone had access to his private space. She'd simply offered him a way to get extra supplies without touching on the subject. He nodded in appreciation and told her his sizes.

"We all have fairly standard preferences anyway." There might've been a smile hovering around her lips. "Monochrome color choices and nondescript everything. When we work, we all try to pass by as unnoticeable as humanly possible. Makes for boring clothing options."

"True." It was a reality made more entertaining by movies. Mercenaries and hit men in black to stand out against the backdrop of other actors in a movie but still seem plausible in the minds of the viewers.

Adam and Victoria both tended to wear shades of grey or navy. They blended with the overcast urban backdrop of Seattle, more casual here on Bainbridge Island.

"We were working in the guesthouse before." Victoria paused, staring at the dry-erase wall. "I think it'd be smarter to stay as close to Roland as possible."

"I don't think he'll mind us taking over this study." Adam lifted his chin to indicate the current room. "There's a couch in here and plenty of floor space. We can make do."

The guesthouse had a bedroom, but neither of them had gone in there. If Victoria was anything like Adam, she'd prefer a firm mattress or sleeping surface anyway. Even hotel room beds tended to be too soft. Left him with an aching back in the morning and waking up with a sense of being trapped inside a marshmallow.

"Agreed. I like being inside the inner perimeter of the area we plan to protect. We've established the outermost property perimeter and the inner perimeter including the guesthouse and main house and backyard pool. We'll set up security for another perimeter directly against the walls of the main house."

He made notes on the board. "We can crash the project timeline some to bring a few of the other security measures online early. It'll take us working in parallel."

Which meant she couldn't spend as much time double-checking his work. Her eyes narrowed but she didn't glare at him. Instead she glanced at her laptop and back at the wall. "Some. Let's bring a few things into parallel, but not sacrifice the level of confidence we have in the system."

He almost chuckled but decided it'd be better not to. Today had been a big step forward in their working relationship, but he was damned sure she would always be the type to double-check both her partner's work and her own. Always.

"We also can't just stay on the property all the time. Too predictable." He had an idea, and it would keep them from going insane too.

She raised an eyebrow at him. "What did you have in mind?"

He turned to face her, crossing his arms and leaning back against a clean part of the wall. "It's all about being unpredictable. We should go off-site once in a while, different times of the day. No need to decide why in advance. Don't even need to do it every day. Just enough to break any patterns there are around here."

She nodded. Anyone posing a threat with enough forethought to start testing response times would be looking for patterns.

"But you have something in mind at the moment." She said it slowly, making her statement something between a question and an invitation.

Oh, he'd tempt her into having fun yet, even in the middle of serious missions. In fact, having this heightened sense of urgency made things even more adventurous. It made him sharper.

He gave her a broad grin, not bothering to hide his anticipation. "I do."

"Mm-hmm." She narrowed her eyes and tapped a fingertip against the casing of her laptop. "If you can come up with enough assurances to implement here for the *short* time we'll be gone, maybe I will let you talk me into whatever this is."

"I'm all for a quickie today." He gave her a wink. Hell, she'd had him so frustrated, it wouldn't take him long at all. But he had more legitimate activities in mind. "I think we can coordinate with Dante for a manual alert system via mobile phones while you and I step off-site."

"Dante." She considered the security lead as she typed a few more notes on her laptop.

He nodded. "Today, Dante. Another day? One of the others. We rotate who we work with, but to start, it'd best be Dante as their lead."

Always good to respect the organizational structure of the security team remaining in place. They were private contractors, after all. There tended to be friction between the contracted vendors and the full-time staff at any place if not handled with sensitivity. Diplomacy wasn't Adam's strong point, but he'd seen how far a little consideration could go.

"Okay." Victoria shook her head. "I might regret this, but the idea is worth exploring."

There was a wistful note to her voice. She was looking forward to finding out what he had in mind. She hadn't made him lay it all out in detail. His lady liked surprises. He watched her with sharpening interest.

As if realizing she'd gotten sidetracked, she shifted in her chair and resettled her laptop. "Let's line up what tasks we're going to complete today then, and get some work done before Roland comes down to check in with our progress."

"Sure." He started to write out a few tasks from memory. He had an idea of what he could accomplish quickly and effectively and what might be better suited to Victoria's expertise. "I've got a few additional ideas to layer into the design too, but let's talk those out off-site."

They'd swept the study for listening devices. Still, it couldn't hurt to go above and beyond with the caution in terms of their planning.

"Uh-huh." Victoria busily typed away at her keyboard. "Keep writing. I'll let you know if there are any tasks you missed."

"Yes, ma'am." He didn't look over his shoulder to see her expression, but her muttered grumbling did his heart good.

She was so much fun to tease, especially as she paid attention to everything.

Experimentally, he flexed his butt.

Her breath hitched. "Try to write legibly."

"Yup." He chuckled. He had a quirky habit of flexing his ass while he was standing around thinking. It gave him something to do, and for the next couple of days, it'd give her something to watch too.

He liked knowing she was watching.

Chapter Eleven

"When you mentioned going off-site, I thought you meant getting in a car and driving into town." Victoria double-checked the spray skirt of her kayak to ensure minimal stray water was going to come in with her.

"Surprise." Adam bent, placing his hands on the end of her kayak and giving it a smooth shove over the surface of the water.

She scowled at him as she drifted past the shallow water, holding her paddle in both hands. Once she was a few feet out, she dipped one end of the paddle in the water and began to propel her kayak clear of the beach. The blade cut the water cleanly, and she moved easily toward the more open water beyond Roland's personal dock.

"It won't take long, and if something comes up, we can grab transportation from town." Giving himself a few quick steps, he propelled his own kayak in the water, taking a risk as he hopped in and settled himself as it was moving. Knowing Murphy's Law, he had about an even chance of overturning his kayak and ending up in shallow, freezing water. But then, anyone in a kayak had to be ready to flip, bail out and get back into the small craft. Adam happened to have a good mix of luck and agility, though, so he landed in his kayak and was able to settle in without getting his feet wet. "Basically, we *are* going into town. We're just taking an alternate route to get a different perspective."

Which was exactly what they needed. Most of the security measures were geared toward intruders arriving on foot or from the road in land-based vehicles. A part of Roland's property had direct access from Eagle Bay. Now that they understood the threat was more dire than paparazzi or angry academics, the water approach became much more important to address.

Her training and experience were mostly focused on land, with some air and water skills. But kayaking was relatively straightforward, and it was a calm day on Eagle Bay. The sky was overcast as usual, and the breeze out over the water was more brisk than it was on land, even right along the shore. They spent a few minutes paddling, Adam in the lead, and much of the tension eased out of her shoulders and back as she warmed to the light exercise.

Sitting low on the water like this was an interesting feeling. She could dip her fingertips into the dark water as her kayak glided across the surface. They'd left the shallows behind, and the bay was deep, leaving her with a sense of a chasm beneath her even if it wasn't open ocean. Ominous as it might sound, her response was exhilaration, not fear. The breeze had a delicious salty bite to it, and the call of sea birds lifted her mood.

Adam slowed to a stop out on the bay, and she dipped

a blade down into the water close at her side to slow and turn her own kayak to stop near him.

"It would be easier for Roland to leave his home, disappear." Adam stared out over the water as he spoke. "I wonder why he's so set on staying here. He's too easy to locate."

Well, this was a very good place to have a private conversation. There was no chance of someone happening by and overhearing them. No possibility of listening devices they might've missed. They'd spoken about the business of protecting Roland earlier, but perhaps here, they could be more candid.

"It would be easier for him to go into hiding." With his funds, Roland could hire Safeguard and fund his hiding indefinitely rather than pouring his money into securing his house. Defense of a single location was a finite plan, most of the time. Eventually defenses would fail no matter how good they were.

"His security lead is loyal, I think." Adam had been reviewing the background checks on each of Roland's personal security. He'd started with the files Roland had but then tapped into Safeguard's databases to delve deeper into known information on each of them. The fun of private contract work was the ever-evolving experience professionals amassed over time. Gathering data on the endless number of players in the field was an ongoing challenge. It helped that each of Roland's men had military background in this case. It gave Adam and Victoria a place to start for them. "Dante has a solid track record for doing the right thing, making tough choices. No red flags to speak of, even if he's made some mistakes along the way."

It would've been more suspicious if Dante hadn't slipped here and there, made the odd bad decision. An absence of those in his record would've been a suspicious void. No. People who were good at their line of work took risks. Taking risks meant messing up once in a while. Dante was a good man and good at basic protection.

"Ray and Brian are decent assets and work best together." Adam placed his paddle across his lap and extended one end toward her.

She took his end and mirrored his move so they could hold on to each other's paddles and remain floating together with minimal effort. It brought him close to her, well within arm's reach. The air was cold enough to bring color up in his cheeks and forehead beneath the brown bronze of his skin tone.

"If they decide to work for or against Roland, it'll be the both of them, not one or the other." She didn't have information to back up her guess.

But he nodded. "I'd agree. We should watch them. They like to play themselves off as Ray being the smarter of the two, but Brian is sharp as hell. For now, they haven't done anything. No red flags. But they haven't been closely scrutinized so far by anyone else."

Well, luckily, there weren't many resources on Roland's staff. Even if they had to keep an eye on Ray and Brian, they weren't outnumbered.

"Jay seems a little foolhardy." She didn't know the man well, but Jay's attitude was enough to put her off and Adam had already expressed a possibility of personal bias against him.

She wouldn't choose a man like that for a team she would be leading. She didn't prefer to lead anything larger than a fire team in any case, preferring to contribute the way she had fit into Gabe's fire team in Centurion Corporation before they'd all become Safeguard.

But just because Jay was a bit of a dick didn't mean he was a danger to their client. "You know him better."

Adam's lips pressed into a straight line. "Yeah. My history with him was under strain. I wouldn't say I know him well though. His people skills haven't gotten better, but I mentioned that to you earlier. I definitely haven't kept in touch with him in recent years. He doesn't seem to have changed much over the time."

She raised her eyebrows. "Is that good or bad?"

"It's not quite right," he admitted. "All of us grow and change over the course of years, or so I'd like to think. Maybe it's wishful thinking for me personally. But Jay has the same attitude, same expressions, same rough edges as I remember from years ago. He's a man full grown, and he doesn't seem to have matured at all from the young people we were when we were active-duty. I could relate to him back then. Now, I don't trust him. It's awkward for me to say, but there it is."

She huffed out a laugh. "I'll admit I find it entertaining to hear you say another man hasn't matured."

He shrugged. "I like to have fun as much as the next person. A little fun can be immature, sure. Jay, though, it's the way he seems to expect things to fall into place for him. Everything. From the small things in day-to-day life, like lunch, and the bigger things—"

"Like better pay, a better job, better opportunities." Victoria tapped her fingers on the shaft of her paddle. "He has a hungry look about him, like he's aiming for those things."

And the man got angry when he saw someone else with what he thought he himself should have. Jay looked at Adam that way. It had nothing to do with Victoria and everything to do with the way Adam walked in and out of a meeting. Adam was Safeguard. He had a position with the satellite company of one of the best organizations in the private sector.

As compared, Jay was no one and he wasn't going anywhere nearly as fast.

"But that's not all it is, is it?" She studied Adam. Confidence, a good helping of arrogance, both covering old scars somewhere deep inside him. She hadn't asked before because there'd been no reason to. People like Adam and her always had history. They'd both admitted it. "What happened where you and Jay came out of the same thing and ended up in different places?"

It had to have come up eventually. Adam had recognized the inevitable as soon as he'd seen Jay the first day they'd arrived. He'd delayed though because he wasn't particularly certain where he and Jay stood at this point either. In his mind, Jay was an old acquaintance. Jay's behavior since had been yet another thing about this entire situation that'd been not quite on target. Adam had hoped to pin down whatever the hell was going on with Jay, but the man hadn't been around to talk to one-on-one.

"Jay and I served together as Marines." Basic information was always a good place to start.

As far as he knew, Victoria hadn't served in the US military, so he'd start simple and get to the complicated part quickly.

Victoria nodded. "Your history as a Marine rifleman is mostly in your personnel file. It's not detailed."

It wouldn't be, at least not the end of his career. The beginning of his service record had been a solid start, something to remember with pride.

"We were in the same unit toward the end. Closer then, all of us were." He and his fellow riflemen had to be, in order to survive. They'd become a close-knit team. "On our last mission, there were some bad decisions made."

He swallowed bile. To this day, he wouldn't throw anyone under the bus.

"Do those decisions need to be discussed for this mission?" Victoria's tone was gentle, with an edge.

"No." His own answer sounded rough in his ears. "What matters is what came after. We lost lives but most of us got out of there. There was an investigation. I was cleared, so was Jay. So were the rest of my team. But we were all given honorable discharges. Our military careers were over. What you need to know here and now is that not all of us took the discharges well."

He'd had a future ahead of him and suddenly it was gone. Ended. It could've been much worse and he'd tried to be thankful, but at the time he'd been so bitter. He'd wallowed in it.

"Ah." There was understanding in the one word. Victoria tucked stray strands of golden hair behind her ear. "Our Jay wasn't happy with his lot. He should've had better?"

Adam nodded. "I was slotted to be a Raider, but I never went to MARSOC. I was discharged. Jay was aiming for one of those slots too."

It would've meant assignment to special operations. Victoria didn't show any puzzlement over the acronym and Adam was glad he didn't have to explain to her. He'd gathered from the level of her experience and the respect she had from her colleagues that she had a strong history too. Not every professional had to have a military career to build the skills needed for this one.

"But he was never even selected, was he?" She'd made a shrewd observation.

Adam hadn't wanted to think about it back then because it hadn't mattered. None of them would go through the assessment and selection. "Neither was I."

Her gaze turned to him and grabbed him, her quiet calm holding him steady out there on the bay. "There is a difference. You may want to forget it but he hasn't. You've made your peace with what happened. I'm guessing part of his grating attitude is because he's carrying a load of resentment. That is important. It makes him less likely to be loyal and more open to opportunities, regardless of the ethics involved. Since then, you went your own way, and he knows nothing of who you've remade yourself into, does he?"

"Probably not." He couldn't be sure. Of course, someone particularly interested could've followed his next steps. He hadn't particularly tried to drop off the map. "I came home to my family here in the States. But I struggled to adjust. Everywhere I looked was the pride in who I wasn't allowed to be anymore. They tried to be supportive, but they didn't know how to handle what had happened, and I couldn't completely explain it for them."

Some of it, he'd never discuss in full with anyone. What he was allowed to say, he didn't want to go into. It was like trying to paint a picture for someone, but having to do it without using primary colors.

"They all knew I'd wanted to go career. They'd known I was slotted to be a Raider. Then suddenly, I had an honorable discharge and a complete change of plans. Or to be honest, I had no plans." Even now, he couldn't look Victoria or anyone else in the eye. He'd committed to this back then, but he'd lost faith in why he'd sacrificed his future for the good of the team.

"What did you decide to do?" Her question wasn't particularly relevant to their current problem. Or maybe it was.

A part of him, way in the back of his mind, came to attention at the curiosity in her tone. She was asking about him, the real him, past the surface of what he could do as part of this mission. If he was going to let her keep him at a distance, as a partner, then he'd give her the bare minimum of details. If he wanted more…

"My father's family is from New Zealand. I still have strong ties to his tribe, and since I needed a complete change, I went to spend time with his whānau." It'd saved him. He looked out over the waters of the bay, drawing peace from the waves and the smell of seawater.

"Whānau?"

He grinned. "Whānau means extended family. Maori people have a wider concept of family than Western European or US folks. Aunties, cousins, and uncles can be as important as brothers and sisters. The ties are strong, and they welcomed me without putting pressure on me to be someone I wasn't anymore."

Victoria's lips curved in a gentle smile. "It sounds amazing."

He huffed out a laugh. "It was. It took a while to appreciate them all though. I arrived and acted like a tourist for weeks. Maybe I was still in denial. Or maybe nothing is a quick fix. But I finally got my head out of my ass. The way of life, the culture, it helped me decide how to redefine myself."

Tension through his shoulders and chest eased as he talked. She was good at waiting, not needing to fill the silence between them or push with a question before he was ready to talk further.

"I learned new skills." He patted the paddles in his lap. "The Maori people have a powerful tradition of whaka, huge ocean-going canoes. Going out in those cleared my head, gave me something to focus on learning, and gave me an appreciation for the peace you can find out on the waves."

He lifted a chin toward the mouth of the bay where it opened to the Puget Sound. It would be good to explore the area. Maybe he could coax her out on the Sound after this mission was complete. There were otters and sea lions to be found here, maybe orca if they were in the right place at the right time of year.

"You mentioned I'd made my peace." He met her gaze, calm and open. "I did. I remade myself."

"Your tattoo?" Her gaze fell to his chest, and not for the first time, his skin ached with the memory of her fingertips brushing over his ta moko.

"Part of deciding who I am going to be moving forward. I had it done once I decided to become someone new. Then I stayed long enough to regain my balance. Applying for new positions was part of it." He'd researched the private organizations and corporations carefully before applying. "Centurion Corporation had several positions, but it was Safeguard's objectives I felt most drawn to. So here I am."

Her lips curved in an enigmatic smile. "You know why you're a part of Safeguard and I do not."

Her admission hit him in the chest. "Seriously?"

"I went with the flow when my fire team spun off from Centurion Corporation to Safeguard as a satellite organization. My husband filed for divorce just before the change in my career, and I've been working my way through that mess." She met his gaze, her cheeks pink with the cool sea air. "I've been in transition this entire time. Then my partner was injured a few months ago and here we are. I was going to work with you through your probation period and decide what to do next. I have options."

"Don't we all?" He took in the woman next to him. The two of them were a pair, in kayaks, floating on a bay with the option to go in any direction. The poetic aspect of it all wasn't lost on him. "When I was a rifle-man, I wouldn't have appreciated all of this."

He swept one arm out to indicate the bay around them, the sky above them.

"But I like where I am right now, here. I very much enjoy your company." He leaned toward her slightly, enough to be within her personal space without over-turning his kayak. "I haven't forgotten how much I enjoy being inside you."

Her gaze didn't waver from his and the color in her cheeks intensified, but the heat in her eyes burned. "Let's get through this mission and consider our options then."

"I'd like that." He wasn't sure he was going to wait quite that long though. "I'll be honest. Patience isn't my virtue. It never has been."

He thought about her too much for patience. He re-membered the softness of her breasts in his palms and the taste of her skin under his tongue. He wanted the strength of her grip on his arms as she held on to him.

"I thought you were remaking yourself." Her eye-brow rose in a graceful challenge.

"I choose how I'm shaping myself moving forward." He gave her his most charming leer and waggled his own eyebrows, making her laugh. He liked her laugh. "Some mischief is good for the both of us, so you'll have to forgive me for being ill-behaved once in a while."

"I might forgive you. Maybe." Her smile didn't fade and it made him stupid happy to see. "On a case-by-case basis."

"All right," he said slowly. "I'll have to make it good for you every time then."

Chapter Twelve

"I am both surprised and not surprised that we were able to get this many components at the electronics stores in this small town." Victoria hefted her backpack.

They'd split their acquisitions evenly. Small electronics packed fairly efficiently, and they both had dry bags in their kayaks to wrap around their packs for added waterproofing for the trip back across the bay. All in all, they'd only been gone a couple of hours thus far.

She'd had…fun, actually. Adam was impressively creative when it came to assembling components for the less conventional aspects of their security enhancements. His delight in gathering electric tape and duct tape to hold together his other finds reminded her of a combination of *MacGyver* and *The A-Team*. He was younger than her, but he'd recognized the TV-show references. At least their age difference wasn't so great that reruns couldn't bridge the gap.

"People living on the island have to do for themselves in bad weather." He walked at her side companionably, exchanging nods with the occasional local as they made their way back to the marina where they'd left their kayaks. "It's not surprising that small electronics and hardware would be well stocked."

"Maybe, but who'd have thought we'd find high-end surveillance equipment?" She had done a double take when they'd spotted those items. The price markup had been irritating, but the convenience of having them in hand immediately versus waiting on an order to be delivered had outweighed the cost difference.

"There's a fair number of affluent people living here." He shrugged. "Eclectic people with the funds to indulge in any number of hobbies, including spying over their neighbor's wall. It's not too hard to imagine."

"Point taken." She chuckled. "Safeguard could probably fulfill any number of small contracts optimizing security for private homes around here."

Roland's property had the advantage of large easements to give him added privacy. His land bordered a park on one side. The other property didn't currently have an owner in residence. The situation afforded Roland with much more peace and quiet than many of the other homes on the island. The thought of all the neighbors peering at each other through the trees between their yards was both entertaining and just a little bit creepy.

"Before we head back, let's have us a feed." Adam pointed at a tiny cabin set at the edge of the water.

"There were any number of cafes and restaurants up on Winslow Way and Madison Ave." She wasn't sure why she was protesting except the little building looked more like a refurbished shack than an establishment for fine food. Besides, there'd been local wine to taste at some of the other restaurants.

"Aw now, don't you ever look for the veritable hole-in-the-wall?" He turned toward her with a mock frown. "Any person who appreciates good food—not fancy, but good food—has to acknowledge that the hole-in-the-wall is the best place to go. Look at all the locals sitting out on the patio. It's got to be worth it."

She paused. He was right. In her travels, enjoyment of food was not the priority. Her mission and survival were. But a person couldn't enjoy life without tasting a bit of the city or town or village if there was even a small chance to stop and enjoy a simple bite to eat. Somewhere in the mess of her divorce and the aftermath of losing her former partner too, she'd forgotten.

"All right, then. We'll have missed lunch anyway."

Minutes later, the two of them were seated at a picnic table outside the shack. A huge helping of fresh clams still in the shell, steamed in a light and savory broth of onions and fennel, butter and white wine, had been piled into a fresh-baked bread bowl. Victoria eschewed her spoon for the moment and nipped up a clam by the shell to taste her plump prize.

"Oh." She sighed happily.

Adam had torn a chunk off the edge of his bread bowl to dip into his broth. "Mmm."

The flavors danced over her tongue, the subtle flavor of the clam going well with the rich, buttery wine broth. The clam had been steamed just so, not too far, as many restaurants tended to do. The result was tender shellfish, not rubbery or chewy in any way. Her bread bowl had a thick, crispy crust and a soft, chewy center that readily soaked up the broth. The restaurant had even provided a tiny container of crushed red pepper flakes, dried by the owner, to add heat to the dish if she desired. Once she'd gotten halfway through her clams, leaving the discarded shells in an empty bowl provided for the purpose, she did sprinkle the pepper over the rest for a wonderful change of taste.

"You like spice?" Adam asked as he did the same, albeit over a smaller portion of his clams.

"I like variety." She took her first clam with red peppers and sucked slowly at the shell to enjoy the added facet of spice to the flavors. "Spice is fun in the right amounts."

He chuckled. "Agreed. Though I've learned to dial back my spice intake for practical reasons."

She paused. "Oh?"

"Well…" His lips spread in a wicked grin and his gaze blazed. "I've found some pepper lingers on the palate, so to speak. While the aftertaste can be enjoyable, the heat can transfer to delicate parts of a partner. If I have hopes to apply my tongue to other tasting adventures, I try not to take on too much burning spice."

The bastard had the gall to wink at her.

She stared at him for a moment, and the image of him looking up at her from between her thighs came back to her. The memory of it had her wet. He was very, very clever with his tongue.

When she didn't immediately deny him, he raised his eyebrows and reached for the crushed red pepper.

Deliberately, he moved the tiny container to another table. Then he continued with his meal.

She should tell him no. They were in the middle of their mission, and she'd been the one to set the expectation from the start that they would be completely professional. Yet this, this play, made the work more of a challenge. It helped her step back and gain perspective on the problems they were encountering in the project. He was keeping her from being sucked so deep into the work that she didn't recognize how to interact with people anymore. He was a magnet.

Allowing this to go on wasn't the professional thing to do, or even the smartest thing. It was unconventional.

They'd agreed together to throw off any watchers with the unexpected.

Anyone who'd worked with Victoria in the past, known her, been with her, would never expect this.

Beyond what people might think, she took in Adam sitting opposite her, fresh and full of the life she'd been too burned-out to grasp. It was so very tempting to allow herself to be swept away in his energy.

This once, this mission, she'd follow his lead. It might show her a way to go about things she'd never risked exploring. Even if it ended badly, she was certain experiencing Adam would be well worth the adventure.

Adam pulled their kayaks onto the small pier on Roland's property and used a hose attached to the small boathouse to rinse them both down with freshwater. Victoria stood clear, her gaze scanning the surrounding area.

She'd been quiet on the paddle back from town. He

hadn't minded the silence, but the heat in her gaze had kept his attention riveted to her the entire trip back. Now, he was splitting his attention three ways: the task at hand, the area around them, and her.

"Lizzy is still covering watch on the main house," Victoria offered in a low voice.

He nodded. It was probably habit as much as anything for him not to talk much near open water. Sound carried easier over the surface and the bay had been calm today. There might be only seabirds and the brave sea otter to hear them at the water's edge, but he'd rather not take chances.

Finished rinsing the kayaks, he took hold of one. She bent and took the other end of it. The kayaks weren't heavy but they were awkward, and it made the job easier with the two of them. In a few minutes, both kayaks were inside the boathouse, resting on racks.

"We made good time." He'd let the door close on them as they'd come in with the second kayak, and the boathouse was dim with only the afternoon light from a small window.

"We're back early," she agreed.

He watched her as she checked the rack again, ostensibly to be sure the kayak was securely placed. "So we've got some time to dally."

She paused, turned to fix him with a long look. In those few moments, she seemed to make a decision. "We do."

Her answer sparked a flame inside him, and it burned through him like a fire out of control. "Not the answer I expected to hear, Queenie, but I am very glad you said it."

"That so?" She didn't come to him. Instead, she drew back further into the shadows of the boathouse. "I'm surprising myself too. Is that a good thing?"

"I think it is." He followed her, giving her time to change her mind if she needed to.

But she was a decisive kind of woman. Her gaze never left his as she bent and untied her boots, pulling them off one at a time. She undid her pants next, sliding them over her hips and down her long legs.

His mouth went dry. The sight of those shapely thighs was enough to drop him to his knees and he didn't resist the impulse. He pressed his hands into the wall on either side of her and looked up the length of her body into her clear blue gaze again. "I'm about to worship you."

Rose flushed at her cheeks. "You're crazy."

He grinned. "I'm eager."

She didn't answer, only placed her hands over his on the wall.

He buried his face into the hollow of her hip, breathing in the spicy scent of her with the hint of sweet. He caught the light musk of her arousal too. Hard to miss considering his position. The hard wood floor of the boathouse was unforgiving, but for this, he'd endure.

He nudged her shirt up to give himself access to skin and kissed her hip. Soft, smooth, he tasted her skin and dragged a few hot kisses along the outside of her hip before kissing his way between her legs.

"You wear some pretty, pretty panties." He nipped at the lace-and-satin bit of fabric keeping him from her.

"I like feeling pretty." Her words came breathy.

He slipped his hands out from under hers, unable to hold off from exploring her any longer. "Let's give you more to feel."

"We don't have a lot of time." Her protest sounded halfhearted though.

He shook his head slowly, brushing the front of her panties with every pass. "We have enough. You're wet for me, Queenie. This won't take long for either of us, but it's going to be good. Trust me."

He was greedy though, because he was indulging himself too. He coasted his hands up her legs from her calves upward behind her knees and along the backs of her thighs. Pausing, he gripped her thighs just under her butt and pressed his mouth against her panties again.

A quiet sound escaped her throat, a needy whimper.

He didn't need another encouragement. He turned and pressed one shoulder between her legs, encouraging her into a wider stance. She gave him the access he wanted, pressing back against the wall and reaching out with one hand to grasp the rack for balance.

"Hold on," he advised. Then he pulled the bit of fabric aside with his thumb and tasted her. Her entire body trembled, and he steadied her with his right shoulder, keeping his left hand on the inside of her thigh to continue to hold the fabric of her panties.

She tasted so good. He started with long licks, making sure to flick her clit at the end of each one. When she squirmed in his hold, he fastened his mouth over her clit and sucked until she choked back a cry.

Still trying to be quiet, which was good. But she could take a challenge.

He suckled and licked more, circling her clit with the tip of his tongue. She writhed against the wall and tilted her hips. He grazed her with his teeth ever so gently, then darted his tongue inside her.

Her breath was coming in short pants. "If you don't come inside me, I'm going to kill you."

He thrust his tongue inside her again.

She was holding on to the wall and the boat rack for dear life.

He backed away, and she gasped, her eyes flying wide open. He caught and held her gaze as he stood in front of her and undid his pants. Taking a condom out of his pocket, he thanked the universe that he was an optimistic man, and opened it. Having her watch him put the condom on was maybe one of the hottest moments he could remember. It was about to get way better. "You only ever have to ask."

Her gaze fell to his freed cock, hard and erect, then rose back up to meet his. "Please."

He lunged for her. They met in a kiss that was more than heat, it was a carnal clash of teeth and tongues. They fed at each other's mouths as he ground his hips into hers. He pressed the length of his cock against her until his condom-covered shaft was probably wet with her need.

He bent his knees and caught her behind her thighs, lifting her. She wrapped her legs around his waist as he cupped his hands under her butt to support her. He nudged at her entrance and slid inside fast, no hesitation. She gasped.

He froze. "Does it hurt?"

She grabbed his shoulder with one hand, the other still holding on to the boat rack, shaking her head. "Good. So good. I want this, now. Hard. Please, Adam."

He lost his mind at the sound of his name on her lips.

He lifted her and slammed her down on his cock, letting gravity help. Her heat wrapped around him, tight. He groaned into her chest. Leaning them both into the wall, he thrust into her again and again, slow then picking up the pace. Her fingers dug into his shoulder, encouraging him. Every stroke shoved him closer to the edge, and he gritted his teeth, loving every second of it. He was going to last, damn it. He was going to bring her with him.

He gripped her butt harder, tilted his head up and caught her mouth in a drowning kiss, as he kept thrusting inside her. She groaned into his mouth, her thighs squeezing his hips. Faster. Harder. Stars shot across the back of his eyes as he lost himself inside her, and she came with him, her core squeezing him as she shuddered in his arms.

They were both breathing in ragged gasps as he let them down slowly to the floor. Trembling from the intensity of what they'd just done, he pressed his forehead to hers.

Victoria Ash. She was an incredible woman. He couldn't get enough of her, the taste of her, the feel of being inside her, but most especially the sound of her voice saying his name. She had his heart and she had no idea.

Chapter Thirteen

"Wasn't expecting to see you out here."

Victoria held up a finger in a motion for Jay to wait while she touched the app on her smartphone, then began walking. This would be the first of many brisk walks up and down the property. She wasn't looking to retrace any of the current patrol routes. Instead, she wanted to clock the time it would take to cross more direct distances. "Oh, we're on-site today and moving forward with the next stage in the implementation."

Jay came up beside her, remaining a fraction behind and to one side. Some might consider it an attempt to stay out of her way. For some reason, she felt more like it was a passive-aggressive move, the way another car might hover in your blind spot on a highway. "You two took off earlier in the day. Roland seemed upset."

The man was fishing for gossip, perhaps, or simply taking the opportunity to speak to her alone. She couldn't decide so she shrugged. "We let him know before we left. There was coverage in our absence."

"Well, yeah." Jay laughed. "We were on-site. We're always here."

Actually, Lizzy had come to drop off extra clothes and a few requested items from the Safeguard caches. She'd found herself a comfortable vantage point on the main house and maintained surveillance from a distance. Lizzy was an excellent sniper and more than capable of providing coverage on the property and their client without ever having to come any closer. Victoria and Adam had put their trust in Lizzy to take out any threat perceived, not the on-site security team.

"You don't have time off?" Victoria attempted to sound politely concerned. Sweet wasn't her usual conversation style.

"Oh." Jay coughed. "We do. What I meant was someone is always here."

Victoria nodded. "Of course. I'm very impressed with Dante's process and procedures here. He maximizes the effectiveness of a small team."

"Him? He didn't do it by himself." Temper colored Jay's words.

Quick to anger, this man. She wondered why she was so tempted to goad him. Considering, she noted the timer on her phone, then turned to head back up to the main house via another approach.

"What, do you need to get steps in on your fitness tracker or something?" Jay continued to trail her, sounding irritable about the choice.

"It's good to know the terrain, even if it is just grass." Victoria decided to be cheerful in the face of his irritability. "Walking in the day is one thing, but there are times when I need to know what the ground feels like under my feet."

He laughed. "You tend to trip a lot?"

"Sure." Simple enough to give him the answer he wanted.

They walked together for a few minutes in silence. Once she reached the house, she glanced up. If she could see the security cameras placed at the topmost point of the house, then they could see her. Happily, she couldn't hear the drones Adam was operating high overhead. Thus far, he'd kept them out of her field of view as she'd been walking. Jay hadn't mentioned them. She decided to take off in another direction, headed for the front gate this time.

"Adam should be doing the legwork for you." Jay clicked his tongue in an admonishing way.

"Why?" She genuinely wanted to hear his answer. After all, most people who made ridiculous statements like that realized how condescending they sounded once the words left their mouth.

"Well, he was a rifleman, he should be out here on the terrain." Jay bit off the term Adam used to refer to his time as a Marine. "Maybe he went soft over the last couple of years, flat on his back on some island getaway."

Victoria snorted. "It was my understanding he was in New Zealand, not the Polynesian Islands."

"Might as well be the same thing." Jay waved away the distinction. "New Zealand is like, basically an island of Australia, as far as I'm concerned."

"Both Aussies and Kiwis would beg to differ." Victoria noted Ray and Brian in the distance, on their patrol of the perimeter. Jay didn't particularly have a reason to be out here either, unless Dante had sent him to see what she was up to.

"Who? Oh, you mean Australians. Yeah. Kiwi though? Isn't that a fuzzy fruit?"

She smiled, truly entertained. "It's a bird too."

The man couldn't truly be so obtuse about New Zealand and their international nickname. Or maybe she was the one being unnecessarily clever. He was definitely bringing out the edge in her personality.

"My point is, I wouldn't be surprised if Adam did nothing but sit on his ass, wherever he went." Jay spit onto the asphalt of the drive, even though they were walking parallel to it on the grass. "After the clusterfuck of our last mission, he had to go hide and lick his wounds."

She'd been curious about the last mission. But then, there were a lot of soldiers who'd left active duty with a history of operations gone wrong on the record. She hadn't been surprised by it. Instead, she'd been more interested in the aftermath. The way Jay was going back to it on his first opportunity to have a conversation with her was a part of why.

It wasn't always about what happened. It was about what people would do to deal with it later.

"Did he tell you?" Jay persisted in poking at the sleeping-dragon topic.

"I've reviewed his personnel files and we've spoken of it to a certain extent." She enunciated carefully, left a pause for him to fill in the silence that followed.

"He sold out his teammates," Jay growled. "He came out of the debrief better than some of us. He had an honorable discharge and recommendations on his record.

He wasn't the lead on that mission, but they acted like he was the one to get us out of there alive."

Twisted truth. It had to be. People like Jay couldn't resist telling the past through the filter of their own bias. Still, she didn't like the implication to Adam's character.

She had to keep her mind open to the possibility that there was a grain of truth that reflected on Adam's character.

"I heard the team made some bad decisions." Offering the small bit Adam had shared with her was more of a prompt than anything else.

"Ha!" Jay's laugh was nasty. "The decisions were the right ones if we'd executed on them immediately. Timing is everything. He was a chickenshit and his delay cost us lives. I was the one who pushed us forward. I'm the reason we came through that."

No one wanted to admit to having frozen in combat. It was an important thing to know about her partner if he might do it again. The question was whether that was actually what had happened or if Jay remembered wrong.

Victoria reached the front gate and glanced at her timer. Turning, she considered what path to take next. She'd had several mapped out, and she'd been walking them at random as she clocked the distances.

"Look." Jay made a play to get her attention again. "You're Safeguard. Badass contract group. You're supposed to be all elite about the pros you hire. I'm telling you he doesn't deserve his service record, not when the rest of us got screwed up the ass for doing the right thing at the time. Anyone can question the decisions made in the field, but Adam should've stayed with us. He shouldn't have gone off plan. It was his fault our mission failed. And he has a history of making changes to the mission plan on the fly. You want that with all your careful planning? He doesn't deserve to be working with Safeguard."

Jay turned on his heel and stalked off, headed for the small security building to one side of the main house.

Victoria watched him walk away and considered what she'd learned about Jay and what she needed to find out about Adam.

Adam directed the drone to skirt around the trees along the perimeter of the property before landing it at the small area he'd cleared earlier in the day by the waterside. Well, he'd been able to track Victoria's movements the entire time without any signals from her to indicate she'd spotted the drone. Testing the drone flight paths in parallel with the manual distance measures had been a success.

A groan rose up from the vicinity of his feet. Glancing down, he saw Tegan had rolled over onto his back, legs splayed in his sleep. The dog had come in to nap as soon as Adam had begun his drone run. It was kind of nice to have the company. He was somewhat surprised, actually, that Tegan hadn't woken when Adam had cursed over Jay following Victoria around during their testing.

She could take care of herself. He had no doubts there. But Jay's behavior had been creepy, clinging. The status of what was between Victoria and Adam remained undefined, and he wasn't the type to need labels, but seeing Jay piss all over her had tested Adam's self-control.

Speaking of piss. Adam looked down at the sleeping corgi. "When was the last time someone let you out to do your business?" It might be a good time for a break, time to stretch his legs, and maybe rejoin Victoria. "Gotta go potty?"

Tegan stopped snoring and opened one eye to regard Adam. Apparently the dog was not going to enable his need to go hover around his lady. Fine. He didn't need an excuse to go find her. He might even confess why he'd gone out to her.

"I had a chat with your friend Jay." Victoria entered the study and stopped to study Tegan.

For his part, the corgi grunted and stretched his forepaws in her direction.

Well, Adam had known she was a direct sort of person but this bordered on psychic. "I saw."

"Good job with the drone, by the way." She stepped farther into the study and leaned her hip against the deck. "He didn't show any signs of having seen it, and I didn't hear it either."

"Thanks." Adam eyed her, cautious. Her arms were crossed over her chest, and her expression was closed off. He was learning it meant her mind was working faster than the words coming out of her mouth. "Jay say anything interesting?"

"To a certain extent. It's fairly certain he doesn't consider you a close friend." She put an interesting inflection on the word.

He scratched his chin. "Man doesn't have to be a friend to work with him. I've been trying to give everyone the chance I hope they'll give me."

She shook her head. "If he were in a burning building, would you go after him?"

"Yes." He regarded her solemnly. "But not because I know him."

Her ice-blue gaze settled on him and held him. "If he ran into a burning building to recover money or valuables, would you have his back?"

Ah, well that was a different question. "Can't stop idiots from their own idiocy."

She nodded. "That clears up a few things, then."

"Where are you headed with this?" He didn't mind questions. They were getting to know each other as they went, but this was feeling like an interrogation.

She sighed and dropped her arms, reaching out to snag a sticky note from the desk supplies. "He was baiting me with what he knew about you. If you didn't know before, you should know if you were drowning, he wouldn't throw you a rope."

Adam hadn't known it was that bad. He'd have given Jay credit for being a decent human being. Based on Victoria's impression, it'd be a bad idea to give Jay his back.

A knot started twisting in Adam's gut. "I want to ask you what he said, but I probably should have a talk with him directly."

What Jay had said could wait for later. What Victoria thought of Adam mattered to him more at the moment.

"You could." Victoria began to fold the sticky note

into triangles. "He doesn't come across to me as the sort who would discuss his issues with you to your face. He's not direct."

It was Adam's turn to sigh. "No. He's not. You're right."

Even years ago, Jay had been a passive-aggressive motherfucker. It'd been like pulling teeth trying to get him to say what he was thinking. More often than not, Adam or their other teammates would hear it from someone else. It was Jay's way. Confront him and he'd find a way to make it look like he'd been attacked instead of constructively working things out.

"I appreciate you talking to me about it." Adam wasn't sure how to pose the question to Victoria, but she was direct. She would give him a straight answer even if it triggered more discussion. "What do you think of me after talking to him?"

Tegan chose the moment between Adam's question and her answer to roll to his feet. He let out a big doggie yawn, looked from Adam to Victoria and padded away. Heading out of the study, Tegan approached the wall in the dining room and stared at…nothing. The wall, maybe?

Victoria placed her folded sticky note on the desk, now in the shape of a small fox face. The movement was slow and precise, as if the paper fox was a delicate thing. Her gaze met his again, serious. "I didn't ask you for details about your last mission. I understand there are some details you can't share. I need to know if you changed the plan of action without warning during the mission, though. I also need to know if you would do it again without telling me."

Ah. The knot doubled in Adam's gut and his stomach churned. He thought hard about what she'd asked. Even now, she was respecting his need to maintain confidentiality on the mission. Most others wouldn't. But she needed his honesty.

"Yes. I changed the plan of action in the middle of the mission. I felt it was the right decision to make to counter situational decisions that were made at the time. They were made in split seconds. No time to consult anyone." A solid team could communicate almost instantaneously and still there hadn't been time. "I acted in the best interest of the team. Some, like Jay, didn't agree. People died."

Old guilt rose up in a wave. Adam tried to give her as much as he could without breaking his word. But how to give perspective without being able to tell her the details of what happened? It was the same problem, and he hadn't been able to explain well enough to his father, his family, the people who'd known him all his life.

"There isn't a day or night that goes by that I don't think of those people. They died. I didn't. It was still the only way to get the rest of the team out of there."

"You acted on your own." Her tone was hard and flat. "Would you do it again?"

He didn't look away from her gaze. "It was the right thing to do. In the future, if I had to, I'd do it again."

The slowly building trust between them broke, tangibly, with his honesty.

There hadn't been any other choice.

Her lips pressed into a flat line. "That's unfortunate."

"Yeah." It really, really was.

Chapter Fourteen

Victoria scowled as she walked the grounds again. The sun was going down and with it, the evening chill was coming in off the bay. The growing shadows created voids where there weren't any earlier in the day.

The obvious time for any attack would be night, but sometimes it was best to strike in uncertain light like the magic hours of dawn and dusk. It wasn't quite dark enough for night vision to be effective and not light enough to eliminate the places where shadows allowed people to hide. So it made absolute sense for her to be out here. Again.

Or at least, she'd use the explanation if Roland or one of Dante's security team asked. To herself, and probably to Adam, she'd admit she was walking off temper and disappointment.

To be fair, he'd been honest.

She didn't know how to reconcile herself with his answer.

"You get the measurements you need or can we lend a hand?" Ray raised his hand in greeting as he and Brian approached. They were still a ways away, but

Ray had pitched his voice to carry. Brian lifted his chin in greeting.

She smiled. No need to acknowledge her purpose outside. If they could tell by observing her, that was fine. It'd be more interesting if they'd noticed the drone earlier too, but she wasn't going to ask.

"This time of day changes the lay of the land." She offered the easy excuse instead.

Ray nodded, looking out over the property. Neither he nor Brian spent more than a glance on her, their gazes constantly sweeping the perimeter. It was their job. "True. It'd be easier with different landscaping. Any plans to clear some of this stuff up?"

"We've made the recommendation to Roland." A landscaping team would be in later in the week to re-move the worst trees and shrubs. She made a mental note to leave a note with Dante so he and his team could expect it as part of the daily schedule.

"All right." Ray simply accepted her comment, no follow-up questions. He was genial enough but not overly friendly.

"Can I ask you a few questions?" It was an impulse and not like her at all.

Ray looked at her straight on for a moment. "Sure."

"If you two were to move on from this posting, would you look for jobs as a team?" She'd noticed their last two jobs had been together. Two was interesting, a third place of work together would've been trend.

Ray barked out a laugh. "Think so. We're brothers."

Victoria studied them. Brotherhood could be claimed in a number of ways. Considering their ethnic background, they weren't brothers by genetics. "Since child-hood? Or through your work?"

Brian gave her a wide smile. It was slightly unnerv-ing, perhaps he didn't smile often. This might've been the first time she'd seen him try the expression.

"We grew up in the same neighborhood." Ray gave her the answer. "My father used to call us One-y and Two-ey. We went to college together, didn't bother fin-ishing, and started focusing on private security. We know how to work together. We might not play as well with others."

It explained why the two of them didn't work with a larger organization. This kind of work allowed them the freedom to work the way they did best.

"Either of you could have opportunities elsewhere." She wondered if she would've considered them in her past work. Possibly. They were both solid, dependable. They'd been conscientious about their job, despite the repetition of their patrols. Neither had relaxed their vig-ilance even if they'd paused to talk with her. In fact, they'd tacitly continued on their patrol. It was she who'd fallen into step with them.

"Yeah we could." Ray chuckled. "But it's not worth being miserable in your job to get higher pay or what-ever. This suits us."

"How do you manage your differences?" She as-sumed they had them. "Ever fight over a lady, food, a work decision?"

The questions sounded idiotic to her, once she let them out. But she truly hadn't ever asked anyone. It had always seemed to be a given in the past that a mature adult could work through those things. But she was zero and two when it came to resolving things with a partner, both her personal life and her professional life seemed to have fails in those respects.

Brian laughed.

It was Ray who answered. "Sure. If it's ever over a lady, it's because one of us is making a big mistake. Otherwise, we generally let things fall out as they will. We don't have the same taste in women, so it's never over the same. To be real, though, we'll throw down over the last soup dumpling."

She smiled. "I'd put up a fight over a soup dumpling too."

"When it comes to business, that happens less often. Dante is a decent lead." Ray considered for a minute. "Generally we don't disagree so much as hold each other's ass accountable for when we screw up."

"That's fair." She thought back to hundreds of times when Marc had made mistakes, more recently Adam. She did a lot of the holding accountable. She was detail oriented and demanding, requiring her partner meet the same high standards she maintained for herself. The idea of ever being caught unprepared or vulnerable was abhorrent to her, so she tended to check and double-check to be sure whoever was working with her never left her open to either of those things. Both Marc and Adam were good colleagues. Yet she couldn't remember Marc ever truly making her consider where she'd made the wrong decision. She wasn't infallible. It was Adam who'd called her out, made her reconsider, talked her into adjusting her planned course of action.

It'd been for the better.

"We try for fair. Sometimes shit happens. If you go for a long stretch where you're never wrong though? You may want to check yourself." Ray rolled his shoulders. "We've worked with those types before, and it doesn't matter what level of excellence a person maintains, it's hella tiring to deal with them every minute of every day when they're always finding a way to twist things so they're right all the damned time. It's like being forever trapped in a statistics seminar."

"Excuse me?"

"The numbers are all there, points of fact, but you can torture the data to prove anything you want if you keep at it. Working with someone like that day to day wears on you, steals your soul."

The bottom dropped out of Victoria's stomach. Her ex had done it all the time, for years. In recent years, she'd lost her patience, her desire to make things work with him, and she'd gotten very good at turning the logic back on him.

The behavior was hers now. She'd taken into herself, and she'd probably worn Marc down with it.

"Work or personal, relationships are between two people." Brian's voice was a deep baritone, gruff and gravely from disuse. "Relationships aren't static either. You want to build a relationship, make sure it grows with you, then it's the decisions of both people to evolve along with it over time. You both have to decide what you're willing to change as you go and whether you're still you as you do it."

She stared at the man with his sleepy expression,

his lids half closed and accentuating the effect of the epicanthic folds over dark eyes. It was like suddenly standing in the middle of some science-fiction movie when the wise teacher archetype imparted a piece of wisdom, then sent the protagonist plunging into chaos.

The ground was unsteady under her feet, and she gave each of them a thanks, a nod, before heading back to the main house to think hard.

Adam was still working with the drone programming when Victoria returned. She paused on her way to the study to glance at Tegan. The dog was lying on his side along the dining room wall in the middle of another nap.

"Seems like an odd place to nap all the time." Her comment wasn't directed at anyone in particular.

Since Adam was the only human in the area, he decided to answer her anyway. "He's generally there if he's not following one of us."

It'd torn him up to watch her go out earlier. It'd felt too much like her walking away. He'd wanted to call after her, take back what he'd said and promise her anything she wanted to hear to keep whatever this was between them going for even a little bit longer.

Instead, he'd kept his mouth shut and let her go work out her thoughts on her own. Better to have given her the truth than to have broken her trust later. Besides, if all he could ever give her was what she wanted to hear, they weren't going to be right for each other as professional partners or something more.

She entered the study and leaned against the desk,

outside of arm's reach. Not the best of signs. "He has a dog bed in the kitchen. It looks new and comfortable."

He glanced up at her, but there was no smile hovering around her lips. Her jaw was clenching and unclenching as if she was literally chewing on the deep thoughts she'd taken out with her earlier. "There are other factors. Maybe he wanted to pick a place where he could open his eyes and see the humans in the household. He can see us in the study and see the top of the stairs from there."

She huffed. "He could just as easily be in the dining room waiting for the next meal. He's always ready for a treat even if he's not allowed them."

"Also a possibility." Adam tried to sound as agreeable as possible.

"He likes you well enough." She leaned forward enough to crane her neck and look back at the sleeping corgi. "He was right at your feet this morning."

"Jealous?" He'd meant it as a tease.

The corners of her mouth dropped and her eyes filled with sadness. "I wouldn't expect him to warm up to me."

Something deep in his chest twinged. "Why not? You like him. He can tell."

"Can he?" She spoke as if her thoughts were far away and present at the same time. Wistful. "I'm not particularly friendly toward him. I'm not even sure I like him. He's a dog. He sheds. But he's always looking like he's got a smile for everyone. Walking the grounds is more tedious when he's not out and about to catch everyone's attention."

They were definitely talking about more than the

dog. Adam didn't mind though. It seemed to him that Victoria didn't have a lot of practice opening up directly to people.

"You don't have to tell him for him to know. Dogs know when you appreciate their companionship. They decide on their own if they're going to accompany you." Adam leaned back in his chair. One of Tegan's big ears twitched and the dog cracked an eye open. "That dog is probably the only absolutely truthful creature on this property. He lets you know what he wants as best he can, and you will know if he doesn't give two shits about you. He's probably also the best judge of character here."

"That's not a comfort." Victoria crossed her arms under her chest.

Distractions were bad, but Adam couldn't help but appreciate the lifting effect the motion had on her breasts. She was unconsciously beautiful and alluring, little effort required.

"It should be. He allows you into his territory without waking. That's some trust." Adam was reaching the end of his understanding of canine psychology, so he wasn't sure how much farther he was going to be able to take this theoretical conversation. He was hoping Victoria would come around, and soon. Otherwise, he was going to have to resort to kissing her into a better mood. Or pissing her off.

She sucked in a breath through parted lips. "I hadn't thought about it that way."

Adam snorted. "Dog jumps up and lands on all four paws, barking whenever Dante or any of the security team comes in. You just walked in without a twitch from him. Obviously, you're one of his."

"What happens if I have to yell at him? Kick him out of the study if he gets underfoot?" She was stretching the metaphor far, really far.

"I guess it depends on whether you let him know you still want to be friends after you finish dealing with whatever was important enough to hurt him in the first place." He figured this was where his own needs could dovetail with the dog's. "It's not always about apologies and who is right or wrong. Sometimes it's about knowing there's a next time to work through."

She raised her gaze to his finally, that striking blue stopping his heart the way it had been over and over for the last twenty-four hours. He wanted to get used to it. Hell, he'd give up caffeine and take this feeling as a daily hit instead. It'd be worth it.

"I guess I've got a lot to learn from Tegan, then." She smiled. "And you, if you'll be patient."

Her smile changed her entire expression from the elegance of sculpted marble to the breathtaking beauty of wild things. He loved seeing her smiles even more because they were fleeting. Almost immediately after she gave a smile, it slipped away, disappeared. All he wanted to do was give her more reasons to smile.

"Well, there's only so much you can learn from a dog. They're straightforward, simple souls that way." He leaned back in his chair, going for a lighter banter. He'd cheered up considerably with her willingness to talk with him more. If she was asking him for patience, they were going to continue to work together. "I, on the other hand, have all sorts of skill sets and ideas to lead you out of your comfort zone."

He watched her carefully. Even if she'd come back with an implied apology, she might not be willing to continue to pursue other aspects of the chemistry between them. As nonchalant as he was trying to be, he wanted to know.

She raised an eyebrow. "I'm not afraid to step outside of what's familiar to me."

Good. He grinned. "Not afraid, no. But I'm guessing you haven't been challenged very often. It's easier to let you take the lead. How long's it been since someone stood toe to toe with you?"

She shrugged. "Present company excluded, most people can't. If they're in my way and I have a mission to complete, I take them down."

He stood. She pushed away from the desk to face him. They stared at each other for a long moment, inches apart. It was more than sharing space, they were savoring each other's presence and he was hyperaware of every breath she took. "We have a mission, but this is outside of it, separate. You can walk away, but you are not going to take me down."

Chapter Fifteen

Victoria steadied herself as she matched Adam's gaze. "I'm not going anywhere."

There, she'd said it. She'd been deciding all this time, struggling with whether or not to let this thing between them go on. It wasn't the right thing to do, but it wasn't precisely wrong either. It was complicated.

She wasn't going to back away from Adam just because it was complicated.

He stood, waiting, a mountain of a man. She wanted to climb all over him—his broad chest and shoulders, delicious muscles and wonderfully bronze skin—but they were on-site with the client. The professional Victoria would've reminded them both of the agreement they had to wait until the mission was over. There was a part of her telling professional Victoria to experiment a bit.

"What's next?" he asked her, his voice low and dark. It was the tone he used with her in the boathouse and in the hotel the first night they'd met. His voice, more so than his question, resonated in her sternum and made her nipples tighten.

She let her gaze fall to his lips, tempting and curved in an incorrigible grin. He could do amazing things to her with that mouth of his. He had devastated her in the best of ways in the boathouse not long ago. Obviously what her professional self considered the correct course of action was already a lost cause. Instead of doing what she ought, she desperately needed to do what she *wanted*.

Lunging forward, she captured his mouth with hers. His arms caught her around the waist and steadied her against him. He opened for her immediately, letting her explore with her tongue and drown them both in the hunger the kiss awakened for both of them. She reached up and cupped his face in her hands as she nipped at the corner of his mouth. He responded by ducking his head and sucking the spot where her pulse beat below the skin of her neck.

She tilted her head back, eyes closed, reveling in the feel of his hard body against hers. "This is going to get us in all sorts of trouble."

She'd kept her voice low. Opening her eyes, she glanced out the doorway and into the dining area where Tegan still snoozed in blissful peace. The dog couldn't care less.

"Trouble can be good." Adam squeezed her butt with both hands, lifting her up and against him slightly.

She pressed her face into his shoulder to stifle her groan. "How so?"

Even though her words were muffled, he'd heard and understood her. He brushed his lips over her ear, nibbled at the sensitive lobe. "Sharpens your reaction time when things take an unexpected direction. You learn to think quick."

He'd dragged one hand over her hip and up her side. His fingers wrapped over the curve of her ribs and his thumb caressed the underside of her breast. Damn, he had big hands.

She sucked in an unsteady breath. "This is a serious risk to keeping our focus."

He shifted, his other hand sliding between them until he cupped her between her legs. His palm pressed against her, moving and applying more pressure until she gasped and clutched at his shoulders. He curved his fingertips until she wished her pants weren't stopping him from entering her. His palm continued to stimulate her clit as his other hand squeezed her breast in a matching rhythm. "Say the word and this stops. Until then, this is going to be all about what you need."

He was going to bring her over the edge, and they were both fully clothed. She opened her mouth to say something—ask, beg, try for logic—she wasn't sure what.

In the other room, Tegan leaped straight out of sleep to his feet and barked, staring up at the top of the stairs.

"Stop." She gulped in air as priorities clashed inside her head and her body cried out for more of his touch, more of him. "I need… *We* have responsibilities. Things. We have more things to finish before the night is over to secure the property."

She hadn't wanted to stop. Honestly, she would've gone where things had been leading naturally, and client site or not, they'd have had their clothes off. The dog had saved them both from an incredibly compromising position.

Adam stepped away from her, struggling every bit as hard. "Yeah. We do."

"But." She dared look up into his stormy gaze. "Once we close out the day, we might be able to pick up where we left off."

It was unprofessional. It was a conflict of several different things. But it was what she wanted with every cell in her body, and if they could do their job and feed this insanity for each other, she couldn't resist giving it a chance.

A wicked gleam shone in his gaze as he leaned in for a lingering kiss. "Let's get to work, then."

It took a few hours to install the new motion sensors in critical locations. They'd chosen key areas not covered by other aspects of the initial deter-or-detect perimeters. These were areas where intruders would seek to bypass the physical infrastructure of the outermost perimeter. Places where the fencing ended at the water's edge and the small dock area were some of their choices and best installed in the dark while the in-house security couldn't necessarily see them.

It also gave them an idea of how much the patrols needed to be altered. If Ray and Brian or Dante and Jay didn't encounter them, then intruders would have as much of a chance to proceed onto the property. They made the necessary notes to recommend to Dante along with suggestions for expansion of the security staff, then headed back up to the main house.

With the new visual security and the drones in place, detection of movement on the grounds from the outer perimeter right to the main house had been significantly improved in the space of twenty-four hours. If they worked quickly, detection directly inside the house was going to be brought up to a satisfactory level before dawn.

"I'm still surprised the stores in town had carbon monoxide and carbon dioxide detectors at a level of sensitivity we were looking for." Victoria carefully marked the spots on the interior walls for drilling, choosing the optimal locations to place the detectors but trying to take into consideration the impact to the interior design. These detection units should be as unobtrusive as possible.

Adam shrugged, following her with a small, powerful drill in hand. "There're some older buildings on the island, and they are used to doing things for themselves. They might not have had them in stock for the same intended purpose as we're using them, but they work with some minor mods with our system."

He marveled at her work ethic. She'd been going nonstop, and it would do no good to suggest a rest. He'd also enjoyed moving undetected over the grounds with her under the cover of night. It'd been good practice and an opportunity to observe her in action.

"Installing detection on the water supply will be more complicated, but I think it's necessary." She stood, stretching her arms and rolling her shoulders to ease the muscles across her back. "This place is not off the grid, and we'll want to know immediately if anyone is trying to get to them via the water supply."

They had sensors to give them the earliest warning possible should anyone try to gas Roland—and them—in the house too. It'd been easy to pick up a gas mask for Roland. They'd gotten creative to set up a safe enclosure for Tegan with a blower unit and filter to provide positive pressure. If a gas situation came up, they just needed to toss the dog into his crate and seal the enclosure. If they had to, they could move him and the enclosure as a whole. Far better and quicker than to try to wrestle an untrained dog into an ill-fitting gas mask.

Roland was their priority, but neither of them had been willing to leave Tegan behind in a worst-case scenario.

Victoria sighed. "This entire wall can't be load bearing. There doesn't seem to be a single stud in the entire thing."

"Well, this detector isn't particularly heavy. We could install it with screw anchors instead of finding a stud." Adam bent to drill the prerequisite holes into the dining room wall. He pressed the tip of the drill to the wall, expecting the same resistance as the others, but almost at contact the wall gave way and the drill point shot through. "What the—"

"What is that?" Victoria was at his side in moments.

Tegan had rushed up and sniffed at the tiny hole made by the drill. The small dog actually whined, his stocky body literally trembling with eagerness.

There was too much air pressure in the wall. Footsteps from upstairs rushed from the direction of Roland's private rooms toward the top landing, toward them. Victoria rose to face their client and Adam drilled another hole, higher and bigger, enough to shine a light and see inside the wall.

"Stop." Roland's voice was tight with anxiety, fear, desperation. All of that wrapped tightly into one word as the man hurried down the stairs.

Tegan didn't go to greet his owner the way he usually did. Instead, the corgi was glued to the lower hole. Something was inside the wall, and Tegan wanted very much to get to it.

Victoria stepped to intercept Roland. "This is not the time to be hiding things."

Roland continued toward them anyway, ignoring the warning in her voice. "You don't understand. This, all this, you'll ruin it."

They froze.

Tegan whined again.

A faint, impossibly quiet shuffle came from inside the wall. Someone was in there. They'd been there the entire time.

"Lock down the house." Victoria gave the order; whether it was to Adam or Roland, it was Adam who rose and moved toward the controls near the front entry. "We need to talk."

In moments, the final perimeter designed to deter intruders had slid into place. Every window was covered with the plates of metal. Victoria had stepped into the study and returned. "The outer security feeds are on loop. They can't hear or see what is going on inside. You have as much privacy as we can give you, but we should go to one room in this house to discuss this. You choose."

Roland was pale, and there was a somewhat wild look to his eyes, but he pressed his lips together and balled up his fists. "The kitchen, please."

Victoria nodded and indicated he should lead the way. Once they were all in the kitchen, she moved to turn on the water at the sink. Adam casually activated a signal-disruption device to ensure any bugs they might've missed in a sweep were useless. He gave her a nod, and she turned the water off again, her motion designed simply to distract Roland.

"Please." Roland didn't require prompting at this point. He was trapped in his own house, had been for a long time. "It was important that no one know, the safest way I could protect us."

Us.

Roland was not referring to him and Tegan.

"Open the door." Victoria was the one to say it first.

Adam studied the walls carefully, realizing the artwork hung on the walls wasn't just modern. Each of the pieces had reflective surfaces, could be small two-way mirrors. There'd been someone in the wall, watching and listening for a while now.

Roland ran his hand along the edge of the lone wall separating the dining room from the sitting area. It stood alone in the house, not joining to any of the other walls. Now that Adam was studying it, he realized it was subtly thicker than normal walls. There weren't any other walls nearby to compare it to, and he'd have assumed it was because the wall was load bearing. But no, it was deep enough to allow a man to stand inside them sideways.

When the door into the wall was opened, they could see precarious stairs leading downward. The wall was a stairwell to a lower level.

"There is no basement in the building plans." Victoria shook her head. "How can we develop a complete security system for you when there's an entire level we didn't know about? It could be a point of entry."

"It's not." Roland said it too quickly. "There's no way out from down there. It's a safe room. No entry or exit except through here."

Tegan had rushed down the stairs as soon as the door was open. It took a minute for their other host to come up. Those stairs weren't easy to climb sideways, the space too close for free movement. The entryway wasn't designed for quick enter or exit. The man was slight with dark skin and hair, and he moved very quietly. Dressed in dark clothes as he was, he emerged from the shadows literally only clearly visible once he'd stepped away from the wall. The corgi rushed up at his heels, the tiny stub that was all that was left of his tail wiggling madly.

This was Tegan's special person. Not Roland.

As the man emerged, he stood uncertainly until Roland held out a hand. Standing together, the two men faced them.

"This is my love." Roland made the statement with quiet pride backed by determination. "You were hired to keep him safe."

Chapter Sixteen

"We require additional clarification." Victoria struggled to keep her temper in check. The result was a cold, flat tone when she spoke, and even Adam flinched.

Roland and his companion deserved it, both of them. Yes, they were standing there as a pair and very vulnerable. But no professional in the world could protect two clients when they didn't know about one of them. They'd set her and Adam up for failure.

It was one thing to take responsibility for one's own failure, but when lives were the consequence, the weight of it would stay with them for as long as they lived.

The new client looked at Roland and gave him a small shake of the head, then stepped forward a half step. Roland did not let go of his hand.

"My name is Manny Okonkwo. I met Roland years ago at a dinner party." Manny placed his free hand over his heart. He had long fingers, aesthetic hands. His high cheekbones were rounded, and his dark eyes held a sharp intelligence despite the weary circles bruising his dark skin. Yet, his full lips formed a gentle smile as he faced her. "I had just taken a position at a biotech company designing and coding for a long-term project."

Biotech company. The words set off red flags and alarms in her head. She wanted to reach for her smartphone and message Gabe at Safeguard immediately. But she needed more information. There were many biotech companies in the Seattle area. The chances of it being the particular company they'd crossed twice now were still small.

"At first my project specifications were so specific, I didn't see how my portions would fit into a particular whole. The potential applications were broad. There were many ways my work could be helpful in support of pharmaceutical device and research studies." Manny dropped his eyes in embarrassment, perhaps, but lifted his gaze to hers again as he continued. "Recently, it became clear that my portion of the code and design was contributing to a weaponized delivery system for a biologic drug. Instead of using my work to help bring lifesaving drugs to patients in need, it would be used to snuff people out of existence. I tried to resign."

It was too coincidental. Worse, someone out there—most likely the Edict organization—had intended for Safeguard to take this contract. Kill two birds with one stone. Recover their wayward asset and discredit the Safeguard team while they did it. It would be payback for the two times Safeguard had upset both Edict and Phoenix Biotech's plans in the recent past. First, when Gabe's fire team had led the recovery effort to locate and extract Maylin Cheng's kidnapped sister from a Phoenix Biotech covert research facility, and even more recently when Lizzy had kept Kyle Yeun alive to testify against Phoenix Biotech in court.

The previous times, the Safeguard team had stumbled across the paths of Phoenix Biotech and their preferred mercenary contractors, Edict. This time, it was too much of a coincidence. It had to have been orchestrated. All the rumors had been the lead-up. This was the trap.

As she remained silent, Adam prompted Manny. "What happened when you tried to resign?"

Manny shifted his gaze to Adam and swallowed hard. "At first they tried to tempt me to stay. They offered increased pay and stock options. When I still refused, they began threatening to ruin my reputation in the professional world. Then they threatened Roland's career as well. This company has far-reaching influence, not obvious to me until they revealed the many ways they could end either of our careers."

Roland scowled. "They could've tried. I couldn't care less what they would say about my work."

Manny squeezed Roland's hand. "No. It would have been horrible. I couldn't stand to see it happen because of me. But something happened. They lost their patience as news broke and the company was mentioned in the press. Legal action was being taken against them. It had nothing to do with me, but suddenly there were no more options. Someone broke into my apartment one night, and I barely got out with my laptop and my dog."

"He called me." Roland's voice was strangled with emotion. "He was hiding in the shadows of a downtown pub, his laptop clutched to his chest. We couldn't go anywhere. It would've been too obvious, too easy, to find us if we ran and tried to check into some hotel somewhere. A white man, a black man, and a dog. We were an easy group to identify just on basic description. Trying for disguises would've been laughable. So I came home, as if I'd only gone out for a drink, and snuck him inside the house here. I had the safe room. I knew it wasn't on any of the building diagrams. I'd never even shown Dante. I told my security team a friend had to leave town abruptly and asked me to watch his dog. I hoped they would think he had run without me."

Victoria sighed. "It probably did buy you time. Then you contracted with Safeguard."

"I knew it would draw scrutiny again," Roland admitted. "But it would've been strange if I'd taken Manny's dog and not behaved in some way to attempt to protect myself. I thought once you were here, once you'd upgraded the security of the property, Manny and I could find a way out of all this."

From a normal stalker or disgruntled employer, probably. They may have had a chance against the average criminal organization, even. "Just to be clear, your former employer was Phoenix Biotech, wasn't it?"

Manny looked back at her in surprise. "Yes."

Adam's gaze shot to her too, then returned to Manny. Ah well, she'd have to bring him up to speed. It was going to be a hell of an initiation for a rookie to the Safeguard team. This was becoming an ongoing feud. Obviously, Phoenix Biotech was equally as tired of Safeguard.

But of course they couldn't simply maintain distance and stay away. No. They had a score to settle, and apparently they'd decided to attempt to take out the Safeguard organization by burning their reputation to the ground.

"Well, the good news is we know what we're up against, then." Victoria was not happy. "The bad news for you is that we are considerably underscoped for the objective we have. Phoenix Biotech employs a private contract organization called Edict. They have questionable ethics and likely have been budgeted to put far more resources in the effort to find you than you've contracted to protect you."

Roland's face flushed with anger. "If you want more money, we can addend the damned contract. This is life-and-death. Don't you understand?"

Victoria didn't move. She waited as Roland fought an internal battle, willing him to harness his anger and fear. He'd need it. Manny, on the other hand, withdrew into himself with an air of hopelessness that made her want to reach out and shake him.

"I understand more about what you face at this moment than either of you do." She didn't bother to cushion her words. She was angry. All of them needed to hold on to the anger and use it to think more clearly. Anger cut through fear. "Phoenix Biotech and Edict can create any number of traps, physical or emotional, psychological or legal. There's no limit to the ways they can tangle you up and give you no way to get free. We have to work together on this in a completely legitimate, documented, legal way. It's what will protect you, us and Safeguard."

Both Roland and Manny slumped, exhausted. It was Manny who spoke. "What must we do?"

She looked to Adam then, because she wasn't about to give orders without his agreement. He was her partner.

Adam met her gaze and the corner of his mouth lifted. He gave her a nod. He was willing to follow her lead, at least until the two of them could discuss more privately.

Relieved, she focused her attention on their two clients. "First, Adam is going to sweep your safe room while the two of you sit and have something to eat here in the kitchen. Reassure Tegan before he wears a bald spot in his fur rubbing against your leg."

Manny chuckled. Roland started breathing again.

"Then the two of you will go down into the safe room if there's space and rest. We'll be sweeping Roland's private rooms upstairs for surveillance devices."

"No one is allowed up there," Roland protested.

Victoria stared at him. "We've been in the house for the last twenty-four hours. Your security team generally has free entry and exit from your house for meals. There's a very good chance your bedroom and bathroom are bugged."

The implication was clear. Despite any background checks and assessments they'd done thus far, Dante's team was under suspicion.

She looked at each of the men in turn, even the dog. "At this point, the only ones I trust to know about Manny's presence are standing in this room."

Adam held his peace as Roland and Manny settled at the kitchen counter with food. When Victoria headed for the study, he followed her.

Reaching out to cup her elbow, he guided her to the

far corner of the room and leaned in close for a very intimate conversation. "Are you serious about sticking to the contract?"

Victoria shivered slightly as his lips brushed her cheek but she didn't warn him off. Her proximity was a heady temptation regardless of the current situation. But here and now, he was focused on discussing their next actions on behalf of their clients. Discussion was going to be a challenge but they could whisper...vehemently, if necessary.

She lifted her chin, bringing her lips perilously close to his. She pitched her voice for his ears only. Even a bug in a nearby fixture next to them wouldn't be able to pick up their conversation. "Absolutely. It's the only way to keep all of us out of trouble."

He couldn't believe what he was hearing. At face value, he'd take those words as coldhearted. But he'd learned a lot about her over a very short period of time. She might not discuss her reasons for the decisions she made, but she was far from uncaring. What was frustrating as hell was her inability to bring him as her partner in on her reasoning.

He wanted to believe, had to, that she would do the right thing by these two men.

"Got news for you. They're *in* trouble. That's how we all ended up here in the first place." His voice came out in a whisper but there were so many emotions bundled up in his tone. Too much, and she'd withdraw from him, keep her own counsel. He didn't want her to shut down on him.

"You don't save a drowning person by jumping in with them," she pointed out.

She took the front of his shirt and tugged briefly. The small contact still sent a zing through his nerve endings. He stared at her, not bothering to hide the desire he was keeping reined in tight, daring her to mess with him more. This was the first time she'd played with him in the middle of business. There had to be a reason. "This isn't you, Queenie. Normally, I wouldn't complain but your timing is shitty."

She huffed out a frustrated breath. "Yes, I'm playing. It's the worst time to do so. But I need your attention on me, what I'm saying. I need you to back away from the edge and think past their plight. We both have to step away from these clients long enough to get a broader perspective." Her gaze dropped to her fingertips, holding the fabric of his shirt. "We need to anchor ourselves so we can take the right steps moving forward."

He still didn't understand what she was getting at. There was no time for this.

"This is love. The real thing. You want to do the right thing? You save this." Adam threw his hand back to indicate the couple in the kitchen.

He couldn't believe she'd hesitate. He couldn't believe she could be so concerned with business that she couldn't feel in this situation. He didn't want to find out he'd been wrong about her.

"Our contract doesn't cover the nuance here," Victoria hissed.

Cold. Hard. The teasing tone completely gone. She'd

dropped it between one breath and the next. Where was the heart he'd seen in her?

"Screw the contract."

"You don't get it." She stepped away from him and paced. She kept her voice low, though, so he had to strain to hear her. "The contract is what protects us and them. It's what keeps our responsibilities clear. We do our job and get out. We don't get tangled up in the aftermath. We can't. None of us can survive the business if we let it happen with every good cause. And trust me, there are far more out there than anyone wants to admit. There is so much good, you can't throw all of yourself into every instance of it. You'll burn yourself out and then one day when an even more worthy cause comes up, you've got nothing left. You have to know where the contract ends."

Adam shook his head, incredulous.

"It doesn't do them favors either," Victoria pressed. "I've never explained this before, and I don't know why I'm doing it now except it matters to me whether you understand me or not. Other people can think I'm a cold, unfeeling bitch, but not you. It matters to me that you understand."

She stared at him, the intensity in her blue gaze pulling him in until his arguments died on his lips. He waited, listened.

"If we get them through this, they have their lives ahead of them. Who will keep them safe? Roland's finances aren't indefinitely going to maintain them. We cannot settle on a solution that would allow them to sit here holed up for the foreseeable future. This contract has an end, and we would be doing them an injustice to let them simply keep renewing it. That's not a good future for them or us. Besides, no defense is good enough for forever. We'd fail them eventually." She dropped her arms to her sides, standing straight and calm, resolution in every fiber of her formidable being. "You want to do the right thing for true love? Think hard, for them, because you better make sure they have an ever-after and not just a for-now."

He stared at her, shocked.

She waited but when he didn't respond she started to pace again. "You suffocate love when you lock it inside to protect it. One day, they're going to lose sight of each other and just see these same walls, that safe room, and they'll hate themselves for being miserable when they have each other. You want a solution, for any love? Find a way for them to be free. Find a way for them to wake up every morning with the freedom to choose to be together and spend their moments of joy together. Love isn't a thing you recognize in a single moment and fight to preserve. It's a forever of choices, repeated, every breath of every day and every night, to be together and share those moments. That's what we need to create a solution for, to give them the chance to make those choices."

He stood as her pacing became faster, more frenetic. This was the first time she'd become unhinged enough to show him her agitation. She was trembling, she cared so much about helping Roland and Manny. She cared.

"I love you."

She froze. "Pardon me?"

He laughed. "You heard what I said and I won't say it again until you're ready to hear it. This time was for me, so I could be sure I said it before we dive into this. I want you to understand that this, this partnership and everything we're about to do, is exactly what I want to do from here on out. I want to work with you, argue with you, take action at your side, and be with you. I want to go out there and help those two men with an eye toward the future, and I want to do it with you, my partner, because damn, woman. You are everything."

She stared at him, her mouth opened slightly and her eyes wide with shock.

After a moment, she found her voice. "You don't make any sense."

He grinned. "Sure I do. You'll get used to it. Yeah? For the time being, let's get to brainstorming."

Chapter Seventeen

"We're finishing up the rest of the security-system adjustments tomorrow morning." Victoria typed quickly on her laptop to transfer notes before Adam erased the wall again. They'd done quite a bit of mind mapping while Roland and Manny finished eating in the kitchen. "I have what information I could pull from our two lovebirds before they were too tired to answer anything more. And you feel the safe room down there is secure?"

Adam spritzed the wall with cleaner. "For now, yes. Roland was right. The only way in or out is that damned narrow staircase. It's seriously claustrophobic getting down there. But it opens up a bit to a decent sleeping area. The two of them are tucked in with Tegan, snug. As long as we can hold the line up here, they are safe in there."

Therein lay the challenge.

For the time being, the house remained locked down. They'd checked in with Dante and explained it'd been part of testing. Dante and his team would continue regular patrols outside. Victoria had pinged Gabe, and they had a conference call with him in minutes on a secure connection.

This was something outside the scope of the project, and they would potentially need backup. The question was how they would handle it officially. She was determined to find a way.

"It's coming up on time, right?" Adam pulled up a chair so he could sit next to her in front of her laptop.

"Yes." She set the laptop on the desk surface anyway.

Bringing up the web conference program, she initiated the call. In moments, Gabe appeared on-screen.

"I'm guessing there's bad news. Why don't you lead with the bad and brighten my very early morning with the new?"

Victoria glanced at her watch. It was indeed a few hours to dawn. She and Adam would need to take turns on watch and make do with a couple of hours of sleep each. At this point, they couldn't risk both going to sleep for any amount of time, regardless of the outcome of this call. She gave Gabe her report, concise and efficient, watching his face for any reactions or tells.

Gabe was a good poker player. She'd known him a long time, but in these situations she couldn't read him if he chose to keep his own counsel. She'd have to wait until he told her what he wanted to say.

At the end of her report, Adam added a few points. They were good observations. All of them were in support of her report, but things she hadn't thought to include. Good for someone who wasn't familiar with Gabe and a fresh perspective.

Adam was a solid partner. He was turning out to be reliable and able to meet her level of detail-oriented. He was also teaching her how to work with someone as an equal contributor. It wasn't easy, but he wasn't letting her run him over either. She needed it. Somehow, their partnership was completely unorthodox with far too much personal conflict of interest, and yet, this was working. She just wasn't sure it could work long-term.

His words from earlier in the night echoed in her head.

He'd meant it. She'd been insanely happy to hear him say it. But she couldn't respond in kind. Not yet, not while they still had this contract to complete. Because it would destroy her if she surrendered to this between them and they weren't able to see Roland and Manny safe.

"This is complicated." Gabe's statement was perfectly descriptive for her internal predicament and the project in general.

"You could say so." She gave him her response in a neutral tone.

The corner of Gabe's mouth quirked. "What support do you need?"

"I don't want this to be a cost to Roland and Manny, not on the original contract and not an amendment." She considered the statement of work. She had it memorized. "But Safeguard members can request extraction at company cost."

Gabe studied her. "Based on your briefing, I can understand why you'd want to save your client the cost. It's considerate but not in the best interest of Safeguard or Centurion Corporation."

They couldn't continue to help people if their generosity drove them into the red. Soldiers of fortune helping those in need at no cost was the theme of a TV sitcom, not reality.

"Deliverables on the statement of work could be considered complete within a couple of weeks, but we have addressed over sixty percent of them ahead of schedule in response to the new developments in the situation. The rest won't be necessary if our proposed changes to the plan are approved. We could reallocate the funds." She'd done the math. The cost could place them at even.

"I'll trust your estimates." The lines around Gabe's eyes relaxed. He preferred it when his team came to him with solutions ready for the problems they were reporting. "In that case, how can I help?"

"We're going to need to take a hit to our reputation." It was Adam who brought up the difficult point. "There are already rumors out there, and we're reasonably sure this situation is intended to cast even more doubt on Safeguard."

There was silence as Gabe considered.

Adam took a deep breath. "It wouldn't be as bad if it were known I was on the project. My last mission failed due to bad decisions on the part of key team members. I am willing to take similar accountability for this situation."

Victoria looked at Adam in shock. This hadn't been part of their planning.

Adam turned to her, his gaze steady. "I could've acted faster in my last mission. I could've influenced the decisions made. I didn't and people died. The best thing I could do in their memory was shoulder the blame for what happened even if it meant the end of my military career. It was the right thing to do then. Here, now, it would be the right thing to do again to see this through. It's plausible. I'm a rookie to the Safeguard team. It would reduce the reflection on the team to a bare minimum."

"No." She didn't even look at Gabe for confirmation. She wouldn't let Adam take the accountability by himself. It would hurt his career in the private sector badly. It could take years to recover, if ever. There were some who would never trust him with sensitive work after this kind of failure. The organizations that would be willing to hire him would poison his soul with the kind of work they'd give him.

It might sound dramatic, but the repercussions of this couldn't be exaggerated.

"I can do this." His face remained serious, earnest. "I'm at the beginning of my private career. I have options. This is something I can recover from."

"You're my partner, you don't do this on your own." She was not going to let him go that easily.

Gabe cleared his throat.

Heat burned her cheeks as she turned her attention back to her commanding officer.

Gabe studied each of them in turn. "Obviously the two of you have cemented into a working team."

His tone was dry.

Neither she nor Adam responded.

"Let's go over the plan. Then we'll talk about the required repercussions for anyone on the Safeguard team."

"That went well." The words came out lighter than Adam felt, but in reality, it was the truth. Their conversation with Gabe Diaz had gone far better than he'd anticipated.

Things worked very differently at Safeguard than he was used to in the US military, or even the way he'd expected a private contract organization to work. When it came down to it, they were business people. They worked for money. The private sector was the evolution of mercenaries in the modern-day world. The Safeguard team might be one of the more ethical groups out there, as was their parent organization the Centurion Corporation, but they still had a bottom line to look to. Resources, weaponry, ammunition and supplies all cost money. The high quality of all of those assets required heavy-duty financial backing.

Even if they did their best to do right by their clients, Adam hadn't expected them to try so hard to work out a solution for a situation like Roland and Manny's. But Safeguard—specifically Victoria—had.

Peace, conviction, were growing inside him the more he worked on this one project. He'd hoped to develop this kind of dedication to an organization again, a team. He hadn't anticipated finding a partner so quickly, and with Victoria, the partnership had so many facets he wanted to explore. He wasn't sure either of them had had a chance to grapple with the impact of it all.

They didn't need to, though, not all at once. They'd handle the current fun now and take the rest a little at a time. He planned to invest whatever it took in time and effort to make it work.

"That was planning." Victoria slumped in her chair. "It's been a long day into night and almost day again.

Everything that happens next is all 'if this happens, then this.'"

Adam stood and stepped behind her, placing his hands on her shoulders. As he gently squeezed the tight muscles, she groaned and sat up just enough to give him better access to her neck and back muscles. "Both of us have to get some rest but you'll never fall asleep this tense."

"Hmm." Her voice was slurred with fatigue. "We'll have to take watches anyway. Anything can happen at any time. We need to be ready to defend or get out."

"I can take first watch." He started to smooth his hands gently over her shoulders, sweeping up her neck and back down in soothing circles. She was too tense to go for the knots in her muscles right away, he was going to have to warm her up some.

She tilted her head forward to give him better access to the back of her neck. "If you keep that up, I'm going to fall asleep right where I'm sitting."

He continued his ministrations, adding light pressure with his fingertips and thumb to loosen her surface muscles. "I'm betting we've caught sleep in worse positions."

"True." She sat with her hands in her lap.

No way was she keeping watch at the moment, so he split his attention between her and the laptop monitors. All was well so far. They needed as much peace of mind as they could get, if not real sleep, to be ready to act when necessary. If they couldn't sleep, they needed the next best thing to reenergize them.

Working on her like this was calming and eased

a tension in him. Minutes ticked on by and he was happy. Happy in a way he hadn't ever been before and maybe he should be worried but he didn't mind at all. He wanted to be touching her always. But they were on the job and despite previous acts of amazing lust, they did need to be professional too. They both cared about their work. He couldn't be jumping her every quiet moment they had, and they couldn't both be distracted right now. But this, the chance to touch her, soothe her, ease some of the aches and pains of the day, this was almost enough to feed his need.

"Mmm." She might've been aware of the noise she made, but he was guessing not.

He chuckled. "Good?"

Her response was inarticulate.

He continued to find knots of tension, pausing to gently roll those spots with his fingers and stretch them until they released. Then he slid his palms over her skin until he found another tight spot and applied targeted pressure again. Every other second, he kept watch on the monitors.

Her trust in him was a growing rush through his system. This wasn't a momentary thing for her. She had completely relaxed under his hands and given over the watch to him. A quick lean forward to get a glimpse of her face confirmed her eyes were closed. This was Victoria, micromanager extraordinaire. He wasn't sure she'd ever done this with a working partner, ever.

She was still upright though, so she was at least partly conscious. But she was resting, and that was important. Dozing, even. He could count on one hand the number of times he'd felt safe enough with his former teammates to doze when they were in the quiet moment during a prolonged mission. She felt safe enough with him.

He used his thumbs to stroke circular patterns on either side of her neck, traveling upward until he pressed his thumbs firmly into the base of her skull. He thought he heard an almost inaudible groan from her, the good kind. His cock jumped at the sound and his pants started becoming tighter.

Down, man. Down.

He shifted the position of his hands to find the pressure points behind her ears with his fingertips, taking the weight of her skull as she tipped back her head in response. As her face turned upward, her long eyelashes lifted and her blue gaze focused on him.

"Time has completely disappeared." She sat up and he let his hands fall away. She rolled her shoulders. "I feel so much better though."

"Pleasure to be of help." He figured it was good to keep his words light. Damn, he wanted her.

"I'd return the favor but I don't think I'd have the same self-restraint." She stood and turned, patting the chair.

He took the hint and sat, quirking an eyebrow at her. "Then can I hope for a fun surprise now that I'm sitting?"

"Yes and no." She settled into his lap and he steadied her with an arm around her waist. "I see no reason for one of us to be standing all night. For the moment, there's no one to see us sharing a chair."

Her firm butt and thighs in his lap definitely blew up the majority of neurons in his brain. "Okay."

Her hands were on the keyboard in front of them though. "Nothing alarming on the surveillance, but is there a chance someone compromised them and we're watching some sort of loop instead of the live feed?"

It happened. The trick was learning to recognize when what they were seeing wasn't the real here and now. Or a sharp technician could layer in preventative measures.

He chuckled. "If anyone tries to hack into the visual feeds I've set up, they're going to get a surprise."

She stirred in his lap, molding her back and rear to the curve of the inside of his body. "How so?"

He reached for his smartphone on the desk. Thumbing the security swipe, he unlocked his phone and pulled up a GIF.

Victoria glanced, then leaned forward slightly. "What is *that*?"

He laughed out loud, then, a full belly laugh. "That is a kakapo. He looks so happy, doesn't he?"

Her shoulders shook as she watched the GIF loop. "Some sort of bird?"

"A flightless parrot from New Zealand." He kissed the bare curve of her shoulder just inside her shirt collar as she continued to silently giggle. "He's a rather lonely soul. He and his bros are from an island in southern New Zealand. Large, flightless and continually calling out to the ladies to come check out their sweet as bowl in the ground for mating. Here's the original video."

He flipped to the original video clip from which the GIF had been created.

She watched for about a minute before covering her mouth with her hand. "Oh no!"

He buried his face into her long hair as he laughed uncontrollably. He'd admit he was giggling maybe, but she wasn't calling him on it. "Oh yes. He climbed up on the photographer's head. And really, he looks so happy!"

"He's..." Victoria spluttered. "His face!"

"The sad truth—" Adam gasped for air "—is both our mole and this parrot will be unfulfilled. There's no actual kakapo females on the island."

She laughed until she lost her breath. "Ah no. You said mole."

He sobered. It'd been on their minds, but this was the first one of them spoke of it out loud. "Yeah. I did. At this point, we have to assume. I put the kakapo response in place on a hunch, but I'm sure someone is going to see it at this point. I can't imagine any other private organization leaving Roland without close surveillance."

"Well, with the house locked down, the mole is going to be dying to know what's going on in here." She stood up, out of his lap.

He missed the weight of her already. But thinking of a mole had him restless too. This aspect of any mission was hard, the wait-but-be-poised-to-make-miracles-happen-when-shit-exploded.

"We've got all the gear set up. We're ready to respond if it happens tonight. Otherwise, we open up in the morning and proceed as if it was just a test." He handed her the controls for one of the drones. "But it never hurts to do more active surveillance if it'll give us peace of mind."

"Thanks." She took the controller. "That cat nap was perfect and I'm too edgy to try resting more right now. I like constructive action. You going to be able to trace if our mole triggers your…kakapo response?"

He grinned in spite of the seriousness of the situation. This was what made this job epic. "Should be able to, yes. In the meantime, we'll use the drones to keep an eye on our patrols, so we'll know who is patrolling and who has the time to be poking around our visual feeds and network."

She gave him a return smile with a predatory edge to it. "It won't be long then."

Chapter Eighteen

"Boom." Adam sat forward in the office chair. "We have a kakapo hit."

Victoria set down the glass of water she'd been sipping. "We could send a drone to see who it is, but I think in person would be better."

Their mole could run and the drones weren't equipped with anything to stop him.

"Agreed." He tapped in a few commands to trace the hack back to the source and log the information for later reference. Evidence was always good to save for later. "I'll go. I had the most recent rest time."

Neither of them had truly slept, but they had switched off watch and light naps between them. They were both as rested as could be considering the situation, and they had the experience to be in ready condition even with the limited rest.

Victoria didn't countermand him. "Go. I'll lock the house back down after you head out and monitor from here. I'll use the drones to keep an eye on who is out on patrol to be sure we've only got the one mole."

In minutes, Adam was outside and headed for the

small security shed. Right there, under their noses. Approaching with caution, he opted to play clueless and see what the mole had to say if it wasn't certain how much they knew about the mole.

As he rounded the corner to the entrance of the security shed, there was Jay, his face red and suffused with frustration.

"All good, bro?" Adam kept his tone light, friendly.

Jay speared him with an angry glance. "What brings you here?"

Adam shrugged. "Out for a supplementary patrol. You know how my partner likes to double- and triple-check everything."

Adam wanted to know why Jay was doing this. No way to be sure Jay would share, not once he knew he was caught, but damn. Jay had it good in this job. Why would the man screw it up? Had the money been that good?

Adam had thought better of Jay.

"Don't bullshit me." Jay spit to one side. "We both know why you're here. I'm not stupid."

Well, no need to play stupid after all.

"Why?" Adam still wanted to know. It didn't make sense to give up a steady, solid paying job for a one-time act of treachery. Jay was going to kill Roland if Jay had a chance, and Manny too. Adam wanted to understand.

Jay barked out a laugh. "Shit. I'm human too. I have feelings."

Adam stared at Jay, wondering where this was going. The look in Jay's face was ugly, personal hate. Very personal. Adam's gut twisted as he realized this, this was what he'd been missing.

Oblivious, Jay started stalking around the security shed. "Since the beginning, man, right from the first day of boot, we were buddies. We got to know each other. And no matter what insane shit we ended up knee-deep in, there you were always saying it could be worse."

It could've been. They'd found out with every new assignment, every new deployment. There was no limit to the nightmares a soldier could face on his next mission. In a lot of ways, Adam had remained sane just by telling himself and his fellow riflemen that things could be a lot worse.

They weren't dead yet, for example.

"And when you talked to me about your life? Fuck." Jay was still going, building up momentum. He kept dragging his hand through the longer hair at the top of his head, giving himself a crazed look. "You've been shafted over and over. The hits just never stopped coming for you."

Family life had been rough. Not rough enough for Adam to have shared with Victoria yet. After he'd been discharged from the military, all of that had seemed to pale in comparison. He'd started learning real lessons in life.

Adam remained still, taking note of the potential weapons in the room. Hopefully, this would fizzle out and his suspicions would be wrong. A crazy thought in a heated moment. But his gut instinct wasn't often wrong. Jay was on a tear, and he was spilling more than a B-movie super villain.

When Jay just kept pacing, Adam cleared his throat. "Life isn't fair. That's okay."

"Okay." Jay laughed again, a bitter sound. "Totally

okay for the universe to be out to get you. Right? Thing is, I don't think I ever screwed you over."

"Never said you did." Adam thought back to drunk nights, any time when he might've accused Jay of screwing him over. He couldn't remember a single time. He'd never thought Jay had. "We're friends."

Jay came to a stop and glared at Adam. "From day one, right? For almost our entire military careers, I've been there to watch your back, hold your ammo, clean up your puke."

"The honors are even on that score, man." Adam watched Jay's face flush with growing rage. He pitched his voice as neutral and non-provoking as possible. "There were plenty of times I had to clean up after your messes too."

Jay waved the comment away. "We were always following your lead. I figured, hell, why not. You had more serious shit to deal with. Even on leave, I took time out from my other friends, my family, my life for you."

Whoa. "I never wanted to take you away from your friends and family. I'm pretty sure if I called, I asked if you had time to talk."

And he had called. The times between deployment had been tough, a struggle to blend with the day-to-day pace of civilian life. He'd called Jay to exchange a few words with someone who got what it was like. There'd never been an expectation for Jay to sacrifice time with his friends and family, his world.

"Yeah, you did ask." Jay was just about spitting words now. "But I could tell what you really meant."

Adam stared at the man. It was like Jay expected

him to be psychic, reading into things said years ago. Or Jay had been the one seeing meaning where there wasn't anything intended. There were layers and layers of perceived bullshit here. Too much to wade through and none of it was actually of Adam's making.

"You needed me, so I was there." Jay slapped a hand into his chest. "I ignored my other friends, my family, my life for you. That's reality. And then when the time came after that last mission, you didn't have my back. I know what you told them."

"I didn't ask you to do any of that." Adam cursed silently. There was no reality for Jay but whatever he'd made up for himself. Even the sequence of events in their last mission had been warped in Jay's report. But Adam hadn't argued at the time, only submitted his own report. The man was so sure he had it right, there was no getting him to see other points of view.

"You didn't have to ask. That's what being a friend is." Jay's lip curled in disgust. "To me, anyway. But friendship is supposed to go both ways. It didn't matter what came our way so long as you were there to cover me."

There'd been no choice. On countless missions, Jay had been the type to engage as soon as possible. He'd charge right into anything. The man had made so many ill-advised decisions, it'd been enough to hold him back from advancement.

Jay's hands balled into fists. "I had just a couple more months. This time I told you I needed you to do something for me, and you didn't want to hear it. You got yourself that honorable discharge and left me there. It was all about you."

"I'd have had to re-up for another two years to be around for your six months. Even if that'd been the right choice for me, it wouldn't have been allowed. The way I was *offered* an honorable discharge, there was no choice." Adam kept his muscles relaxed, his joints loose. He wasn't going to show any body language that might set Jay off and take this from a verbal vent to a physical outburst.

He didn't want to have to take out his former friend.

"Yeah, it would've sucked." This time, Jay literally spit on the floor between them. "But when you boil your reasoning down to what's best for your future career? What the fuck? What does that say about our friendship? Suddenly all that time living through hell is just business."

"I needed to support my parents. Pay off my dad's hospital bills." Adam tried to keep his tone even. He was not going to escalate this insanity, especially not while Jay had at least one gun on his shoulder harness. "Military pay is enough for a single person, but it wasn't going to be enough to keep them in a home."

"I'm a single-income household too." Jay's volume went up a notch. "Paying for a wife who didn't love me and two kids. I had to make sure they had food, clothes. I wanted out as much as you did."

"We're both out now." Years could be a lifetime. Adam wasn't going to deny it. But here, now, they were both standing hale and whole. He couldn't figure out why Jay was so damned mad.

"Yeah. You went home and cleared up the issues. Then you went off to fucking New Zealand for god knows why. I came home to divorce papers and all of my fucking belongings piled on the curb." Jay leaned forward slightly as he started shouting. The tendons stood out on either side of his neck as he lifted his fists. "While I was sorting out the mess in my household, eating hot dogs and ten-cent noodles, you were off rubbing noses with exotic hotties on the other side of the world."

Adam set his jaw. He'd explained the hongi to Jay, just as he had to Victoria. The difference was, Victoria had absorbed the small tidbit about a foreign custom with delight. Jay hadn't understood squat.

"And your dad had cancer." Jay settled back on his heels, sadness in the droop of his shoulders. "I feel for you on that. I do."

It wasn't a good sign.

Jay growled. "You got shafted but I had problems too. And it pisses me off that you couldn't be bothered to hang around to help me. I have a right to my pain too. I thought maybe someday, after I did my best to have your back, you'd have mine. But you didn't. You left. You didn't do shit for me."

Adam dodged to the left as Jay brought his gun up to point directly where Adam had been. Before Jay could adjust his aim, Adam crossed the distance, stepping inside his guard. Grabbing Jay's wrist with one hand, he lifted his other arm and slammed his elbow into the side of Jay's neck. Adam's forward momentum continued as he kept control of Jay's gun hand, forcing Jay to stumble backward.

As Jay went down, the man tried to tangle his legs in Adam's. Adam lifted his feet and stepped around Jay, going down with him and trapping his gun arm in an arm bar. Legs on either side of Jay's shoulder and arm trapped, Adam lifted his hip until Jay's shoulder and elbow strained.

Jay released the gun.

"You fucker!" Jay was screaming. "You always made it about you, never me."

Slender legs came into view, out of range of Jay's flailing legs. Victoria stood there, her own gun aimed at Jay.

Her hands were steady and her gaze was cold. "You are immature, self-absorbed, delusional, and quite frankly, a brat in big-boy boots."

The red haze began to clear, and Adam tore himself away from the edge of doing something he'd never forgive himself for doing, like permanently dislocating Jay's arm. "I should kill you, Jay."

Jay laughed. "Sure. Of course. After all I've done for you. It'd be all about what you want to do, right?"

"Adam." Victoria's tone was as pleasant as if she was asking for another lump of sugar in her tea. "This is actually a decent time to let him know what you really think. Get it all out. I doubt he'll have visitation rights where he's going."

"What?" Jay struggled, but Adam switched his hold and flipped Jay on his stomach. In a few seconds, Adam was securing Jay with hand ties and duct tape. Even a former Marine wasn't getting out of it.

For a second, Adam considered turning away. Just call the police and let it be over. But then he'd be replaying his thoughts inside his head for the rest of whenever and never get the closure of having given Jay the chance to hear it.

Jay wouldn't want to.

But there was Victoria, she'd opened up as they'd worked together. She'd made herself vulnerable, and it had made her stronger. She was the partner he wanted and lancing this festering bullshit was as much for her understanding as it was for his peace of mind.

"Never about you?" His own words resonated in his ears in a growl. "Let's talk about our first leave off base. I let you share my hotel room because your reservation got fucked up. And yeah, I met a girl and brought her back to the room while you were at the bar because you were entertaining a flock of chickies on your own. When you tell the story, you never mention how you brought three of those back to the room in the hopes of getting laid."

It was petty. It was inconsequential. It felt hella good to get out of his system. Victoria raised an eyebrow.

"Do tell us more." Victoria chuckled.

Jay's face was almost purple with rage.

"Let's talk about the pictures you showed all our bros from our hike out to Red Rock Canyon. You loved to show them to the ladies. Big, bad rifleman out in the rugged wild. You're wearing boots I fucking gave you. You're holding my boot knife in those pictures like you're some kind of badass while I was on the other side of the rock holding the ropes to keep your ass on the side of that rock face." Adam wanted to spit now too, but he didn't.

These were stupid events, tiny moments of time in his memory. They should've been fun and happy, and they'd been twisted into toxic thorns in his side because Jay had gone on bitching about them over and over again. Adam had never defended himself before this. He'd never spoken up for himself. He'd just let Jay paint a crappy picture of him with Jay's version of reality. No more.

"I..." Jay craned his neck from where he was on the floor.

"And phone calls? Let's talk about the times I stepped out of briefings to help you think through issues with our CO. Or maybe we can recall the times I took a call from you on patrol because it'd be too long to wait until I got off duty." Bitterness welled up as Adam brought each of those points up. Things Jay always seemed to find a way to needle him with in some passive-aggressive way. Adam was a direct kind of guy, and he was going to get it all out and be done with it. "Emails? Let's talk about how many emails I read for you. I burned brain cells making suggestions for a more professional approach, and what do you do? Ignore everything because someone else told you those emails were just fine."

Jay croaked with his face still half crushed into the floor. "My emails are professional."

The absurdity of the conversation snapped Adam the rest of the way. He didn't care if all this was petty or insignificant. It felt good. Finally.

"Including things like 'shit hit the fan' and 'bust ass' and 'clusterfuck' are not professional correspondence." Adam literally laughed at Jay. "You don't tell a commanding officer you only get to fuck me up the ass without my permission once."

Victoria joined him in laughing, even as her gaze held steady on Jay. "You can't be serious."

"As a heart attack." Adam took a deep breath and let it all go. "Let's talk about how many times I gave you an assist with a technical issue. How many times I hopped on the phone so you could rage about the chain of command and how they treated you after one of your ill-advised emails."

"Tch. Sounds to me like a drowning man trying to drag the person next to him under too." Victoria's assessment was delivered in a matter-of-fact tone, all the more devastating because it was completely without heat.

Jay screamed in inarticulate rage. Then, panting, he started laughing. "You two keep talking. Talking and talking."

"Oh, we will. This is good for the both of us." Victoria was unconcerned. "You see, I manually sent out the call to the authorities and requested backup from Safeguard. They are en route, and we're just passing the time waiting for them."

She switched to a one-handed grip on her weapon for a brief moment, dropping her near hand to her side, out of Jay's line of site. Her hand started in a fist, then three fingers pressed along her thigh. The next moment, she had her gun steady in both hands again.

Three. Three hours. It was a long time to stall, even if it was therapeutic. And Jay was stalling too. Timing was everything from here on out.

"I left the military because it was time for me." Adam let some of the sadness he'd been keeping locked up filter into his words. "What's the word going around the internet, Victoria? Gaslighting? You were gaslighting me, Jay. Every effort I ever made for you, everything I ever did for you… It was like it never happened in your brain."

"You were sabotaging my career!" Jay's voice cracked with outrage.

Never. "No one has time for that. I left the military and didn't look back, man. I didn't talk to anyone. There was no way I could undermine you."

"Liar. You're nothing but toxic." Jay was testing his bindings, flexing his arms and wrists, looking to loosen the ties. He wasn't making any progress.

"If there was any toxicity, it was all in your head, born of your perception." Victoria calmly kneeled, resting the weight of her knee into his spine as she aimed her gun at the back of his head. She'd apparently decided the therapy session was over. Adam was inclined to agree. "Anything you thought happened to you came out of your insecurity and your decision to lash out at Adam to protect yourself. That sort of thing backfires on a person. Call it karma, if you like."

Before they wrapped this up, they needed to know the timing Jay was working toward. It was imperative to find out when he was expecting his reinforcements. It'd be close, and they had to time it to take their next actions just a fraction late. Too late and they all were truly dead.

"Think hard, Jay," Adam advised. "You did all that talking behind my back hoping I'd never know it was you. You ruined your own career with your bullshit.

There's no one accountable but you. It's not me against you. It's not the universe. It's just you. Grow the fuck up."

"You're wrong." Spittle came from Jay's mouth and his eyes were glazing. His face was turning red.

Victoria eased off his spine slightly, ready to react if he turned on her.

"How long can you stall?" Adam asked the man. "Maybe if you breathe deep and slow, you'll have enough time. Or you could tell us how much time you need, and we might give it to you. How long until Edict is on top of us?"

Jay's face twisted into an ugly scowl. "When you told me you were leaving, it was the biggest bitch move I've ever seen in my life. Now? You come here, needing my help to secure this place? You're worse than a stranger as far as I'm concerned because you napalmed the fuck out of that bridge."

It'd been an outside chance to get Jay to tell them the timing outright. Neither of them had built their plans to be dependent on it.

"You're out of time." Jay's laugh was ugly, his chest heaving as he arched up despite his restraints. "Curl up and hide, man, because this is going to go bad for you. So bad. It's going to be all over the media, and no one is ever going to want to work with you or your precious Safeguard ever again."

"I just rolled my eyes so hard, I might have seen the back of my own head," Victoria informed Jay with a straight face.

"Nah, bro. Nah." Adam shook his head, clenching his jaw against the pity rising up as a sour taste in his mouth. "That was your way. You hid inside your own head and gave yourself the comfort of lies to survive when the truth scared you, like it might kill you. You've always protected yourself however you could, even when it meant hurting people around you, not just pushing them away. You always had a reason, still do, for why the shit you pulled was justified. You did things to make sure you took out your competition before they could hurt you. But when those people rose up despite you, it was the universe that wasn't fair. It couldn't ever be your fault or your failing."

Adam stood as Dante, Ray and Brian loomed in the doorway. They'd been listening. They showed him empty hands. None of them were a threat.

Adam focused on Jay. "You don't want truth. You don't want fair. You want everything, and it's a damn shame because it means you won't ever be happy. And even if you succeed in getting everyone out of your way, so you're the last man left standing on the field of competition, you're going to feel awful and exposed. Why? Because you are a piss-poor representative of the human race."

It was Brian who came in first and jerked Jay up to standing by one arm. Ray joined his partner in securing their former coworker.

Dante held up his smartphone, showing the feed of their entire exchange to Jay. "Don't even try to talk your way through this."

"My becoming the scapegoat for your ill-advised jack-assery didn't help you back then." Weariness washed through Adam at the thought of the wasted effort. "Now? Go do your time and hate the world. The only difference is this time, I'm not going to have the future guilt of having left you out in the world to hurt more people."

"Local authorities are on the way." Dante stepped into the tiny building. "Victoria briefed me on next steps, and we'll head to the gate to turn him over. We'll all be clear when the shit hits the fan."

"Good." Adam rolled his shoulders to release the last of the tension. Letting loose like that had been cathartic. Embarrassing, but therapeutic. They'd needed the time. "Thanks for your help."

Brian and Ray dragged Jay past, and Brian paused. "The fuck was that parrot about?"

Adam threw back his head and laughed. "I'll send you the video link."

Chapter Nineteen

Victoria reentered the main house, Adam close behind her. She headed straight for the kitchen as Adam hit the control panel to lock down the house again. The metal panels came down across all of the windows. He even moved furniture to barricade the front entry.

She ran her hand along the corner of the dining room wall, opening the tiny passage. Tegan emerged first, happy to see them and apparently well rested. The dog's perpetual grin brightened her mood. Roland came next with Manny close behind.

"This next part is going to take a lot of trust," Victoria told the two of them. "Follow our instructions exactly. Don't argue. Don't hesitate. We are cutting this close."

Roland and Manny nodded. They'd had a chat earlier in the day. It was Roland who cleared his throat. "We're ready to give up all this."

Manny gave her a smile. "I disappeared once. We can do it together this time."

"Good." Adam threw them each bulletproof vests he'd retrieved from Dante's supply closet.

Once both men had them on, Adam fitted Manny

with a pet harness. He adjusted the straps so it settled high on Manny's chest.

"Tegan goes in this. It is imperative to keep his head level with yours." Adam tugged the harness harshly, making sure it wouldn't slip.

They'd have no margin of error for the dog so once he was strapped in, that was it. The rest would be luck.

Roland started to say something but an alert beeped from the study.

"Time's up." Adam said and bent to scoop up Tegan.

With luck, the small dog would stay calm strapped to Manny.

Victoria headed to the study to check the surveillance. As predicted, Dante's team had reached the gates and headed out toward town, to turn Jay in to the local authorities. No sooner had they left than new company arrived, not of the friendly persuasion.

"They're coming," Victoria called out. She activated the small personal comm she was wearing and carefully enunciated. "Initiate evacuation protocol to bravo extraction point."

"Copy." Adam's voice came back to her via the tiny earbud she wore.

Their communications were up and operational. She typed in a brief command on her laptop to send out a distress call via the property security system to alert local authorities.

In the house, Adam had rushed upstairs and raised a commotion as he tossed the beds and opened the special "emergency kits" they'd created while they waited during the day from gathered supplies.

Roland and Manny waited in the dining room, away from any windows.

Victoria strode to them and handed them each an unmarked container. "Take these carefully, splash every window frame. Don't get any on yourselves."

"Is this safe?" Roland asked.

She glanced back at him from over her shoulder as she began to splash the hallways. "No."

Adam came back down the stairs. "It's jet fuel. A present from Safeguard. Non-combustable, but when we light it, it will burn hot and bright for one hell of a show."

"This is a good idea why?" Manny was splashing the window frames as instructed, Tegan strapped to his front safely so the man looked like a two-headed person.

"It'll be hard to see anything but this house when it goes up." Adam took the containers from them and proceeded to douse the front foyer. "It's our best chance to proceed to the extraction point while the fire obscures the lines of sight from the main gate."

Victoria had her weapons lined up on the desk in the study alongside Adam's. She began arming herself with the rest of her arsenal, above and beyond her normal conceal-and-carry. Her small pack had waterproof bags with GPS, burner phones and backup ammunition.

"Everything from here on out will happen quickly, and it is not going to be fun," she warned Roland and Manny.

The first had gone pale. The second nodded grimly.

"We are in your hands." Manny took hold of Roland's, and the two of them waited for her next orders.

Adam returned from the foyer. "Ready for initial contact."

They gathered in the study. Adam had his laptop open and a drone aloft to provide supplemental vision. Just as well.

Two trucks were coming up the small private road. One slowed, allowing the lead truck to approach the exterior gate. The lead truck stopped just shy of the gate interface.

Four people, a fire team, poured out the sides of the truck. Each member moved quickly, taking up a firing position in strategic locations with direct view of the gate and the main house far beyond.

The driver had remained in the vehicle.

"That truck is probably armored." Adam shook his head. "I'm surprised they didn't bring unmarked black SUVs. Would've made the same statement."

"Trucks are more common on the island," Roland offered hesitantly.

Victoria paused, then reached out and gave the man an awkward pat on the shoulder.

Adam watched and spared her a small smile. She made a face in return. She was working on her people skills, and obviously it was a work in progress. As for Roland, he was going to be all right.

The driver rolled down the window and reached for the gate intercom. He didn't even make any pretense. "We can make this easy."

Adam snorted. None of them moved to give a response. Instead, Adam patched a clip of video taken earlier in the day of Roland pacing in the front foyer and staring at the front door.

The truck driver kept his finger on the gate intercom. "Look, we already know you're in there."

A pause. A muttered "Target confirmed."

The microphone on the gate intercom was better than the truck driver knew, though they didn't need to hear his mutters to anticipate the next moves. The waiting fire team shot out the obvious security cameras that had been a part of the old system. They also took out two of the newer infrared and night-vision cameras installed in less obtrusive spots.

These people had some knowledge of the initial stages of the security upgrade, thanks to Jay.

Adam sighed. Finally he pressed down the space key on his laptop and leaned forward. "Last chance to back away."

The truck driver hit the gate intercom again. "This is your last chance, Safeguard. All of you are done."

"I'm sorry." Adam looked to Victoria.

Solemn, she nodded.

Adam toggled a set of switches he had set up to wires extending off the desk and out the one window they'd left open. To the people in the room, he said, "Charges one and two blowing, get low, get low, get low."

Victoria pulled Roland and Manny down into crouches.

Land mines planted all around the gate area went off. The speakers erupted with the sound of the explosions, bringing the sound right inside with them. When the air cleared, the area around the gate was still. The lead truck lay on its side. No movement.

The second truck pulled forward and a second fire team disembarked, immediately opening fire with a non-targeted surpassing fire.

"Fully automatic weapons." Adam stood from his chair and grabbed his pack, slinging it across his shoulders. "They are very determined to take us out."

"This is Edict, they can't afford to come out of this without their mission objectives complete." Victoria met the gazes of Roland and Manny where they remained crouched. "It's what we're counting on."

Victoria went out the window first, ensuring there were no other trespassers on this side of the property. There would be, she was sure, but they hadn't come this far yet.

Adam stood at the window, keeping an eye on his laptop screen as the remaining Edict fire team progressed forward cautiously. Now that they'd encountered land mines their little mole hadn't warned them about, they were taking precautions. It would give Adam and Victoria the time they needed to proceed to their next phase.

She gave the signal for Manny and Roland to follow her. Once they made it out the window and onto the ground beside the house, she pulled them away from the cover of the house wall and into a nearby dead zone created by a gathering of landscape shrubs Victoria had hated. When they were hidden from the house, Adam picked up a pair of incendiary grenades.

"This won't burn as much as we'd wish for," he warned her over the comm. "Not enough furniture for fuel."

"Copy." Victoria responded. "We'll have to hope the doors and basic structure are enough. Kayaks are waiting."

He turned then and tossed the grenades, one at the front door and one up the stairs. Then he dove out the window.

"What?" Roland was starting to ask as Adam reached them.

Both Adam and Victoria overrode him. "Go, go, go!"

They put as much distance as they could between themselves and the house, reaching another dead zone and diving into the partially excavated ditch where a large tree used to be. When the house went up, the sound of the explosion was tremendous. The oxygen in the near vicinity thinned and air rushed past them toward the house, clearing the scent of burning fuel and tempting them with the smell of the bay instead.

Victoria led the way, running toward the waterfront, crouched as low as possible.

Adam shoved Roland and Manny ahead of him.

This was the not-so-fun part of the plan. The open ground stretched in front of them, and while their enemies didn't have clear line of sight on them, they definitely didn't have the time to get line of sight on their enemies.

As they approached the water, Roland panted. "There were only four more, right?"

Victoria shook her head.

Behind them all, bringing up the rear, Adam hurried them down the length of the dock. "There will be eight more people at least, maybe ten. Those were just the ones that came to knock on the front door."

"Eight more?" Roland's voice had gone faint.

Victoria didn't take the time to turn to check on him. Adam would let her know if the man was falling behind. She kept her gaze front, watching the night for shadows that didn't belong.

Adam's voice came low and quiet. "Minimum. We know Edict has at least one sniper too, but we don't know if she is deployed on this mission."

Considering the last two instances where Safeguard had crossed paths with Edict, Victoria was guessing not. The sniper in question had a conflict of interest with the Safeguard team and Edict wouldn't risk her unpredictable behavior.

Besides, Safeguard had a sniper too, and Lizzy was out there in the dark. Somewhere.

Victoria spoke into her comm. "Twenty-five seconds since contact. Was the flame enough?"

"We're alive." Adam's response was terse.

There'd been no contact from Lizzy. If she'd encountered Edict, she might not initiate comm. The worst fight imaginable was a sniper versus another sniper. If it was going on, they wouldn't be engaged with the rest of the activity on the property. They would be engaging each other.

"Best to assume we are on our own." Victoria sent out a silent hope for Lizzy. They'd worked together before, and the not knowing never got easy.

"Well, shit." Adam wasn't used to it yet. Maybe he hadn't worked with a sniper in his unit in the past.

They hustled along the length of the dock and into the tiny boathouse at the end.

Roland was gasping for breath now. "This, I don't understand. Shouldn't we be taking one of the motorboats? Aren't you supposed to get us out of here safely?"

"You need to get down," Adam advised.

"Why? The house already blew up."

Secondary charges in the safe room went off and up on the hill, the main house ignited a second time.

Chapter Twenty

"Stay here." Victoria pressed Roland and Manny in the doorway, sheltered from any vantage points. The approach up the dock was clear but there were trees to either side.

Adam stepped back outside the boathouse with another unmarked container.

"More jet fuel?" Manny asked.

She shook her head. She didn't blame him for asking. "No, this fuel will burn more normally. The kayaks are smaller and we need them to burn for a long time."

"But—" Roland started, thought better of it and stopped.

In the distance, weapons fire proved they hadn't taken out all of the fire team that'd approached the main house. Either that or another fire team was approaching. She shoved the two men back into the boathouse and pressed them flat on the floor.

Adam dove in, cursing, as the long-distance-weapons fire hit the boathouse. Wood fragments flew and from the cursing around her, every one of them had taken damage.

"Anyone seriously hurt?" she asked, but pushed herself up to check Roland and Manny over herself. Manny had curled on his side rather than lay on top of Tegan, and the dog whined at her, giving her palm a brief reassuring lick.

The dog was up for sainthood.

"We have two," Adam said, his voice audible within the boathouse and on her comm.

As two men breached the boathouse, Adam pressed another remote trigger and a claymore exploded at the end of the dock, sending the other two in the fire team flying.

Victoria stepped into the lead enemy's guard, closing with him in close hand-to-hand.

Adam took down the second man, the two of them grappling on the floor.

Tegan let out a short bark and Manny wrapped his arms around the brave corgi. Now was not the time.

A gun skittered across the floor as Adam disarmed his opponent. Victoria cursed as she saw Roland pick it up, but she had to focus on her man. Each time he tried to strike her, she trapped his hand or forearm and returned a quick blow of her own. At this close range, she wasn't able to get enough power behind her hits to be definitive, but she was able to keep him off balance and drive him back and away from Roland and Manny. She trapped his arms twice more, finally creating enough space between them to get a good right hook in to his jaw. In the split second it took for him to recover, she lifted her leg and drove her foot into the inside of his knee. The man went down with a scream.

A gun fired and Adam grunted. His opponent slumped to the floor.

"Is he dead?" Roland asked.

"No." Adam disentangled himself from the other

man. "And thanks, but don't ever shoot in the direction of a friendly ever again."

His movements were stiff and her heart stuttered inside her chest. His shoulder, clear of the bulletproof vest, was slick and shiny. Roland had shot through Adam.

Adam's gaze met hers. "I'm fine."

Victoria knelt, unable to look at Roland for the moment. There was no time to think on Adam being injured, no time to pause. She'd have to trust him to get through this. She *could* trust him.

Instead, she reached for the heavy iron ring and pulled up the trap door.

Adam pulled a semiautomatic off one of the prone men on the floor. He turned to one side and began firing randomly in short, controlled bursts. Then he turned and did the same in the other direction.

"What are you—?" Roland's voice was edging toward high-pitched panic.

A man came up through the trap door and Victoria shot him, point blank, in the head. His eyes didn't even have time to widen behind his scuba mask. "We're making it look like the fight is continuing much worse than it is."

She stepped down through the entry. No other opponents. The diver had been a just-in-case sentinel, not part of a fire team. She reached up and tugged at Manny.

In moments, Roland and Manny were with her, treading water beneath the boathouse.

Adam was doing a good job of simulating a firefight above him. Moments later, the kayaks floated away from the dock and went up in flames. The waves pulled them farther out into the bay.

Victoria reached for crates tied under the boathouse

and untied them from the pilings. She shoved them out in various directions, letting several float before setting loose others.

Finally, she gave Roland and Manny each one. "Keep these between you and the land. Swim with me. Watch Tegan's muzzle. Keep both your heads above water."

Manny wasn't having any trouble swimming and Tegan's short legs were working in the water as if the little dog was helping. She had no idea if the dog would know to hold his breath should Manny have to go under, but she was hoping for the best here.

As they floated away among the other crates, Adam entered the water. He let loose more crates, then tossed something up into the boathouse before diving below the surface.

"Crates, stay behind the crates." They were far enough out, but she was taking no chances.

The boathouse went up as the grenade exploded. More fire obscured line of sight as they swam.

It wasn't hard for Adam to find them. He knew where they were going. As he approached a set of crates, harsh breathing told him he'd rejoined the group.

"It's me." He swam close behind one of their clients.

"D-d-d—" Roland was close to losing it.

Adam swam close and helped the man keep his grip on the crate. "We've got you. Not far now."

Far out over the water, the kayaks were easily visible as the flames lit the night. Dark shadows made their way across the destroyed dock toward the boathouse. But they'd find a mess of equipment and wreckage. They'd have no idea if there were bodies.

There was enough of an undertow with the tide going out that they wouldn't ever be sure if the bodies had gone out into the deeper part of the bay.

Long minutes and hard swimming went by, but they reached a sheltered area along the shore of the neighboring park. Sirens in the distance announced the approach of local law enforcement. Edict would have to withdraw.

Roland was a shivering mess. Between the cold of the water and shock, the man was going to need attention as soon as possible. Adam rubbed his hand in circles between the other man's shoulder blades. "Soon. We're almost clear."

Once they were safely within cover, Victoria sat Manny on the shore. The man had pulled his knees up, his arms around Tegan. The small dog looked the worse for wear.

Moving quickly, he helped Victoria open the crates. Unwrapping the contents, they spread out the inflatable kayaks and started the pumps to get them ready.

As she got their two clients settled in the kayaks, he set about obscuring any prints or other tells they might have left behind. In minutes, they were floating out over the water, paddling silently and following the cover of the shoreline. The flames of Roland's property faded as they put distance behind them.

Victoria's voice came across the comm. "Alpha team clear. Ready for extraction."

"Copy that, Alpha team." Another voice came up on the comm. "We have you. All clear."

Chapter Twenty-One

"You cut that close."

Victoria nodded. Seated in the infirmary at Centurion Corporation's training facility outside Seattle, she waited impatiently for the tech to finish cleaning up the variety of small cuts and abrasions she'd acquired in the night's activities. Lizzy stood at the opening in the curtains. The infirmary only had one or two other patients from random training incidents, but the curtains allowed for a measure of privacy.

"Where are the others?" She almost laughed at herself. Adam. She wanted to know where Adam was, but they were still partners, and with this mission to close out, she needed to approach everything as professionally as possible. Besides, after Adam, she did want to know how Roland and Manny were faring. And Tegan.

Though when the Safeguard team had come for the extraction, the corgi had seemed to be in the best shape of all of them. He'd been a ball of wiggles and licking people and making new friends. That was one lucky dog.

"We put Adam in a private room because of his gunshot wound." Lizzy stepped into the area as the tech finished up and left. She pulled up a stool and sat. "It looks to be fine. Being in the cold salt water of the bay cleaned it out and kept bleeding to a minimum. He's just getting an IV as a precaution. It'll take maybe another hour for the bag to finish."

"Good that it's not worse." She'd worried. It hadn't kept her from carrying out her part of the mission, but it'd tugged at her attention. Compartmentalizing her concern to a back part of her mind so she could focus on her objectives had been harder than ever in her experience. She'd even had lovers on her teams in the past, and none of it had distracted her like this.

It was going be a problem.

"We'll be looking for a full debrief later, but for now, how was Adam on this mission?" Lizzy was watching her carefully.

Victoria gave her colleague, her friend, a level gaze. "He's an excellent asset. Detail oriented. Good soft skills working with clients and potential partners."

Lizzy smiled. "Good. So we can set him as your permanent partner."

"No." The word ripped something inside her, but Victoria pressed on. "He can't be. We're going to need to partner him with someone else."

Lizzy's dark gaze flicked toward the door and then back to Victoria. "Are you resigning?"

Victoria had thought hard about this. She hadn't been sure she'd been a fit for Safeguard anymore. This mission had proven to be awkward. But she'd grown. With the experience she had and the years behind her, she hadn't grown this much in a project in a long time. It'd stretched her in ways none of them had anticipated. She didn't want a command position, and the Safeguard organization paid her enough. "I was considering it. I wasn't feeling particularly challenged by the current missions we had lined up."

Lizzy raised a single eyebrow at her. "Your partner came back with a hole in him. You look like you took on death by a thousand paper cuts and survived. The both of you blew up the client's property—multiple times— and ended up with a covert extraction from the mouth of Eagle Bay. It's a good thing there's shark-eating oc- topi in the Puget Sound or you all may have attracted more than just Edict's attention tonight."

"Obviously this mission was subject to scope creep." Victoria sighed.

"Scope creep?" Lizzy didn't bother to hide the in- credulous rise in her tone.

"Significant scope creep." Victoria glared at her, dar- ing her to try to claim it was anything else. "The as- sumptions in the original statement of work did not cover the extenuating circumstances at all."

Lizzy laughed. "I should make you write up the con- tracts from here on out."

Please no. Never. The idea of a desk job was stifling.

"I appreciate a good contract to keep the mission clear, but I'll pass on the change in responsibilities." Victoria plucked at the medical tape holding a stupid cotton ball to the back of her hand. They'd taken blood for testing while they'd patched her up to be sure she hadn't picked up anything alarming from splinters or random bits of metal or bay water.

"Not fair." Lizzy pouted. "Gabe didn't give me a choice."

"As I remember it, you didn't argue much." Victoria hadn't minded the adjustment in the organization. She'd agreed that the structure of the teams had to change from fire teams to duos. "It's not that I don't want to work with Safeguard anymore. I just can't have Adam as a partner."

Lizzy's dark eyes took on a gleam. "Yet you said he was exemplary. If there's nothing wrong with his performance, are you requesting he be assigned a different partner because you had the chance to assess his potential in…other aspects?"

Victoria narrowed her own eyes. "Don't be obtuse. Yes. I want to be with him. Which means I can't work with him. It'd drive us both insane. We'd botch up our work and potentially end up dead. It's a mess."

"It's a wonder the two of you came out of this in such good shape, plus with an extra client."

"Don't forget the dog." Victoria snorted. "I must say, it was significantly harder to come out of there with a furry animal that requires oxygen. Your goldfish is the only other mascot for the office at the moment."

"Are you keeping the dog?" Lizzy sounded alarmed.

Victoria shook her head. "I have no idea what Roland and Manny will do, but it's my impression they plan to take Tegan with them."

Lizzy let out a sound of relief. "I was about to ask if you'd taken a hit to the head too. You were sounding massively changed by this mission. Definitely not yourself."

"Is that a bad thing?" Victoria winced at the vulnerability in her tone.

There was a long pause.

"If you want to continue doing what we do? Yes." Lizzy had always been painfully honest. It was one of the reasons Victoria asked her for her opinion. There was little reason to make oneself vulnerable if the feedback was too kind to be constructive. "Owning a dog or other pet, having dependents, is hard in our business. Our schedules are too variable. We make too many enemies to care deeply. It's dangerous to give pieces of ourselves to vulnerable souls. It puts them in danger."

Of course. Victoria had been the one to teach teammates those lessons in the past. The truth of it still resonated in her chest, despite the cold ache it left in her gut.

"That said, it's not healthy for us to be alone either." Warmth touched Lizzy's words.

Victoria's lips widened in a smile despite her caution. "Adam is not a vulnerable soul. He would be in danger far more often than your Kyle or Gabe's Maylin, but he wouldn't be who he is if he took a desk job."

"Neither would you." Lizzy tapped the side of the hospital bed. "I'm very glad you haven't asked for your role to be changed to a desk, even if it would be fantastic to have you in charge of contracts."

"I'm not certain how to ask, but I will. Where possible, can our relationship be taken into account when missions are assigned? Time together would be appreciated." Though, for her part, time away would be equally important as she and Adam explored what was between them. If she had the assurance it could work within Safeguard, then she could talk to him about their choices. And hopefully, he hadn't changed his mind or his heart about her.

"We'd have to take your relationship into account." Lizzy sighed. "There's no need for an official policy or anything, but we wouldn't assign you to the same mission considering the conflict of interest. I do think the nature of our missions will be evolving so there'll be time to think it through."

Victoria nodded. Her heart sank. The decisions Adam and she had made would result in serious repercussions for Safeguard. "How bad is the damage?"

"Safeguard was mentioned in the newscasts covering the destruction of Roland's property this morning. It being mentioned with a definitively negative spin." Lizzy chuckled. The sound of it wasn't precisely evil, but it wasn't right either. "Gabe has ideas on how to handle it. Kyle gave him a few suggestions. My man has a scary mind for business."

Victoria perked up. "That sounds promising. Really, being truly good guys was rather boring."

Adam sat, staring at his IV, wishing the drip would go faster. There was almost nothing more boring to watch. Waiting for water to boil and golf tournaments came in as similar experiences.

There was a perfunctory knock at the door before Gabe filled the doorway. "Congratulations."

Not encouraging, when Gabe had delivered the word in a neutral tone. No clues in inflection or expression to give Adam a direction or hint of how this debrief was about to go. "I wasn't aware that congratulations were in order."

He winced. It was very likely the response would be that he should be.

Gabe chuckled. "You're alive. Your partner is alive. And contrary to the current newscasts and reports from the local authorities, your client is alive plus one additional person and the little dog too. Since that was the plan, I'd say your mission objectives could be considered a success."

"Has there been a public response from Safeguard yet?" There might've been. It was Gabe's prerogative to issue a response in the best interest of his organization. This debrief could be to let Adam know how Gabe and his superiors had decided to handle the situation. It could result in termination of employment, maybe a refusal of recommendations. Adam would be at square one, beginning again. It'd be even harder to get a position with a different private organization. It'd probably be shadier, with few ethics and a lot more moral decisions for him to make. He'd have to make compromises in order to stay employed.

He sat up straight, despite the irritation of the freshly cleaned bullet wound in his shoulder, and decided it was okay. He'd made the right decisions back there with Victoria. These were the consequences.

"No. We won't be making a public response to any of the news outlets." Gabe came farther into the room and shut the door, then stepped over to lean against the side table. "As far as the outside world is concerned, Safeguard is business as usual. This was just another contract, and we are not at liberty to discuss the particulars. Discretion is part of the reason our clients trust us."

Wow. The way Gabe had said all of that, Adam would've been pulled in too and led to wonder if everything hadn't happened exactly as contracted. Which was intended, of course.

"I'm glad Safeguard has a plan for handling the public relations after this." Adam chose his words carefully. Next steps could still be rough for him, but maybe if he could negotiate, Victoria would be free to continue the work she enjoyed with her team.

"You'll be receiving a bonus in addition to your salary. Your probation is also officially ended, and you are confirmed as a permanent employee of Safeguard. Welcome to the team." Gabe held out a hand.

Adam stared at the proffered hand. "Excuse me, could you clarify?"

"We're happy to have you as a permanent member of Safeguard if you still want to be a part of the team." There was definite amusement in the other man's tone. Gabe's hand remained extended.

Reaching out, Adam took Gabe's hand and gave it a firm shake. "I'll confess. I'm still confused."

"You're also fresh off a mission, short on blood and sleep, and coming down off the heightened awareness we all maintain to stay alive." Gabe made it sound like Adam had the common cold. "The med techs were very clear with me when they realized I was coming in to talk to you. Our techs tend to fuss over us. You'll get used to it. There's also nothing official or contractually binding for you to sign, so I didn't feel it was an issue to have this talk here and now."

"So let me get this straight." Adam stared into Gabe's very serious gaze, watching for any tells, any signs of duplicity or a trap about to be sprung. There was nothing but patience. "My first mission went completely off the rails. But you're taking me off probation and I'm a permanent member of the team. To my understanding, Safeguard's reputation has been under scrutiny and this is going to reflect very badly on the organization. But, you're giving me a bonus?"

"Yes."

Panic hit Adam and his heart pounded in his chest, betrayed by the stupid monitor hooked up to him so the entire room, specifically Gabe, could hear his reaction. "Victoria is not responsible for this by herself. She shouldn't take accountability, not for what I talked her into doing. Please, don't let her."

"Calm down, Mr. Hicks." Gabe glowered for a long moment while Adam struggled to remain seated on the hospital bed, literally gripping the edges to keep from grabbing his commanding officer and shaking him to pieces. The bastard actually grinned at him. "We could have used either of you as a scapegoat. I gather you're familiar with how it could've played out. Blame the failure of the mission on the questionable decisions of an individual. Ensure they disappear quietly and let the public furor blow over until everyone has forgotten the unfortunate incident. It happens. Sometimes there's no alternative. Fortunately, Safeguard has some creative minds."

Adam's mouth had gone dry. But he was following, barely. Victoria must be okay. Gabriel Diaz was saying she hadn't taken the fall either. There were no scapegoats in this situation.

This team hadn't sacrificed one of their own.

"We're using this opportunity to be more discerning in what contracts we accept." Gabe rolled his head and a few vertebrae popped. "When we first started, it'd been advisable to take on some of the more publicly sparkling engagements. Bodyguards for the people with the right contacts, political figures, and wealthy had been key to securing funding and gaining immediate exposure. But none of us wants to babysit celebrities for the rest of our active careers. Now, you and Victoria have done a fairly spectacular job of demonstrating the concentrated impact of just two resources on a limited budget. The visual results are reasonably spectacular and the actual outcome is sufficiently mysterious. We needn't make any public statements."

Gabe chuckled as Adam's mouth fell open.

"Celebrities and social butterflies won't touch us now. Too rough, too dangerous. They are sufficiently outraged to take their business elsewhere."

Adam tentatively grinned at Gabe. "And the real players are starting to reach out to us, see what we can do on more challenging contracts that need a certain level of discretion."

"Which we've demonstrated admirably here."

Adam shook his head. "I wish Victoria and I could take credit for the level of genius."

Gabe shrugged. "You each have good instincts. We

have other minds for making the most of what happens next. This will mean higher-profile work, off the grid. The missions we'll take will be covert and likely international. They'll still lean toward protection and personal security."

"Sounds good to me if it does to Victoria." Adam wondered if she was nearby, in another infirmary room or resting someplace else.

"About that." Gabe waited until Adam met his gaze again. "You'll be assigned a new partner at Victoria's request."

Chapter Twenty-Two

Victoria was waiting when Adam arrived at the cabin. This was the larger residence on the Safeguard property for extended recovery. Originally, the entire fire team had stayed here: Gabe, Lizzy, Victoria and Marc. Marc's room was empty. Gabe and Maylin stayed in the nearest small guest cabin on short retreats, now that it'd been repaired from when it'd taken explosive damage during Maylin's initial time with them. Lizzy rarely made use of her room since she and Kyle preferred to stay in Seattle or travel on their time off. Today, it was just Victoria…and Adam.

He strode down the long hallway, past the kitchen, and came to a stop when he spotted her.

"You have a choice of rooms," she told him quietly.

His face was neutral as he took a few more steps toward her, his dark eyes churning with some strong emotion. Trouble was, her nerves told her it could be any number of negative things. Her heart hoped for better. Her mind tended to tell her heart not to hope, but this time, she did it. She hoped. He'd convinced her of the good things a positive attitude could create.

"There are empty rooms," she continued. "Or, mine is here."

He turned his head, looking past her into her simply appointed room. The main characteristic was a very comfortable king bed. The only other furniture was a simple desk for her laptop. Everything else was shoved into a closet.

"Gabe tells me you've requested a new partner." Adam's voice came out hoarse.

Ah. They were going to do this in the hallway. "Yes."

"Why?"

It was her turn. She needed to tell him how she felt, what she wanted. And then she needed to ask him if he'd agree. But the words rushed up and stuck in her throat. She'd never been good at asking for what she wanted. She could defend what was already hers, and she could stand against anyone trying to take something from her, but asking was new.

Here she was, fresh out of a divorce. Her ex-husband had decided she was a coldhearted bitch and hated her. Her former partner had decided not to continue in their career field, and his empty room was just down the hall. Life moved on, changed, and she was trying to define new steps forward.

It was terrifying.

"I know how to do my job well. So do you." She needed to put a question in somewhere but explaining came easier. "From a practicality standpoint, it makes more sense for each of us to train new partners."

"So you're staying with Safeguard too." He took a step toward her. His posture was a challenge. He wasn't approaching her with caution. That wasn't his style.

"Yes." She glanced past him down the hall and back to him. No one else was in the building. She should be able to ask him, but she was still stuck on the information exchange. It was steadier ground. "Lizzy briefed me on the change in direction the organization is taking. I like it."

Adam covered another few feet. He was standing right in front of her at this point. "I don't have a lot to go on, but celebrity and political clients weren't all that exciting to me. Transitioning to more covert assignments sounds interesting. But, Victoria, why are you giving me a choice of rooms?"

She had to tilt her head to look up at him. "There's always a choice. There's several rooms."

"Including yours?" His gaze searched her face.

Maybe he wouldn't make her ask. From the beginning he'd looked past the surface with her, had the patience to dig for what she couldn't put out there on her own. "Yes."

His lips spread in a slow, wicked smile. "Permission to enter, Ms. Ash."

She stepped back, giving him space to step inside her room. He did, filling the small area with the power of his personality and a tense awareness she savored.

Questions. She had questions for him. It wasn't fair to make him dig for what she was thinking all the time. If she wanted this, she needed to meet him halfway. "How is your shoulder?"

He dropped his bag against the wall. "I'll show you if you show me your injuries."

"I…" She was caught off balance. "Minor abrasions and contusions, nothing serious."

He lifted a shoulder and dropped it. "Same. I still want to see. Don't you?"

Swallowing hard, she nodded.

His gaze never left hers as he shrugged out of his shirt, revealing his broad chest and shoulders. The one shoulder was minimally bandaged to protect his bullet wound. The bandaging was clean, no signs of bleed. The medical tape didn't even obscure his tattoo. His ta moko.

She took a step toward him, until she was well within arm's reach. "Your ta moko, you said it was done in New Zealand, when you were redefining yourself. What do the symbols mean?"

He held out his hand. She looked at his open palm for a moment and placed her hand in his.

"This." He lifted her hand until her fingertips brushed a central symbol with a double twist. "This is a pikorua. It's for growth and the joining together of two different things in life. For me, it was growth but I'm hoping it will be a joining moving forward."

She parted her lips. The edges of the marking were raised on his skin, permanent and purposeful scarring of the skin as part of the tattoo. The texture fascinated her, the same way it did whenever she ran her hands over his body. Her fingertips wandered, and he let her explore. She traced a repeating angular pattern. "And this?"

"Pakati." Adam's voice was turning husky. "It represents a warrior, past battles, the courage and strength it took to survive."

Her fingertips continued, the layers of meaning in

his ta moko revealing a story to her that she'd already learned. "This?"

"Ahu aha mataroa. For new challenges, because I decided I still have a lot of living to do."

Yes. She sighed, happy. "New challenges. Will you be with me? Try staying with me as a new challenge?"

He lifted his hand to cover hers, pressing her palm over the entirety of his complex story. "It would be an honor."

She smiled up at him, and words scattered from her brain as she met his gaze. This man, he did everything to her.

Stepping forward, he leaned close until his forehead and nose touched hers, both at the same time. He stood still with her for a long moment as they breathed in each other. "This is the hongi. We exchange the ha, the breath of life, as we share our souls. It's a greeting among the Maori, and Victoria Ash, I am very glad to have met you."

She reached up to cup his face in her hands. He leaned into her palms for a long moment before she closed the small distance between their mouths and pressed her lips against his. They both took their time, enjoying the warm pressure and hint of sweetness between them. Then he growled low in his throat and nipped the corner of her mouth. She opened for him, savoring the moment his tongue swept in to explore before letting her own dance with his. She wrapped her arms around his neck, pulling him to her as his arms circled her waist.

Heat ignited between them. Not that it had ever been gone since the first time they'd met. It'd been there, banked smoldering coals of desire and mutual attraction, burning deeper as they'd fallen more and more for each other. She wanted to gasp for air and be consumed by what they ignited in each other, over and over again.

He lifted her, burying his face in her cleavage as he did. She held on as he walked the few steps to her bed and dropped her on it. She was unbuttoning her pants as she landed, gratified to see him getting out of his clothes with the same haste. Buttons undone, zippers down and fabric was tossed aside until she lay naked in front of him and he stood by the bedside gloriously nude.

"You are a beautiful man." She couldn't help it. She wanted him to cover her like a blanket. Then, maybe later, she wanted to climb overtop of him.

"I'm an impatient man." He loomed over her, his hands coasting over her body, caressing and gently squeezing all along the way.

She closed her eyes and tilted her head back, enjoying the rush of sensation as he explored the surface of her body. The slight roughness of his calloused palms, his strong grip, his achingly gentle touch as his hands skimmed over her more sensitive parts.

She bit her lip as he coaxed her knees apart. He paused for a moment, long enough for her to open her eyes and look down her own body to see him poised just between her thighs, staring up at her. Their gazes clashed, and he ran his tongue along her slit in a long lick.

She'd never heard the noise she made. He didn't give her a chance to think about it. He feasted on her, licking and nibbling at her, and she watched. He drove her insane and she watched him do it. When he clamped his mouth over her clit and sucked, she gasped and almost lost it, but he released her, lifting his head. "Where else do you want me to put my mouth? What else do you want to feel?"

She swallowed hard. "I want to feel you inside me."

He leaned down, angling his head, and darted his tongue inside her.

She bucked. She couldn't help it. Tease. Two could play. She lifted her hand and cupped her breast, squeezing just a little. "And I want your mouth here too."

He grinned at her. "I love when you tell me what you want me to do."

Climbing onto the bed, he leaned over her. As his mouth closed over her nipple, wet and hot, he slid two fingers inside her.

She cried out.

He sucked her nipple with the same rhythm he used to pump his fingers inside her, and she writhed. She moaned. She grabbed his head and held him to her. He kept up the suction and the pressure until her entire body convulsed with the power of her orgasm.

She sucked in air as he stroked her through the aftershocks, prolonging the exquisite pleasure. When she could see past the stars again, she narrowed her eyes at him. "You are a dangerous man."

He pressed between her legs, reaching down to take himself in hand. He pressed the tip of his cock against her, sliding it up and down her slit and circling her sensitized clit with his tip. "You drive me beyond temptation."

She reached down and grasped his hips. "Come inside me."

He pressed into her, stretching her in the best way as he sank in balls-deep. They both groaned. He shook his head and planted one hand on the bed just above her shoulder, bracing her. With his other arm, he hooked her leg high up. The position opened her wider to him and tilted her hips for even deeper access.

"Hang on," he muttered.

She wasn't sure if he was talking to her or to him but she tightened her grip on him.

He thrust into her then, and she shouted. It was good. So good. He picked up the pace, pounding into her and they were both calling out. Over and over until her lower entire body tightened, ready to crash over the edge again.

"Adam!"

He groaned. "Say my name again. Louder."

She did.

They both came, hard and intense, holding on to each other through it all.

It took forever to come back to themselves. Or maybe it only took the better part of an hour. It could've been a few minutes. She had no sense of the time, and really, she didn't care, because the minute they both recovered, she planned to be on top of him to send them back into the same state again.

He leaned over her, his voice only barely unsteady, tracing idle patterns on her skin with his free hand. "So we'll stay here?"

"For a few days of earned rest and to orient you with the facilities here." She smiled up at him. "Then it's back to Seattle. We'll have to see what the next contracts will be."

"That's the business side of it. What about us?" He dropped a kiss on the bridge of her nose.

She tipped her head to one side. "Well, we've never seen each other's flats. It could be fun to spend some time in each."

He nodded. "Could be an adventure."

She smiled. "I would like to share, eventually. We'll see what our time is like between assignments."

"I'd like to take you back to New Zealand too. I'm betting it's been forever since you took a vacation."

She narrowed her eyes at him. "And you just started working with the team. We might hold off on a vacation for at least a few months."

He chuckled. "True. It'll be fun, working all of this out."

"Seeing what works for us." She drank in the sight of him, leaning over her. This was right. Felt so incredibly, fundamentally right. The two of them were vibrantly alive and so much more than the existence she'd led before she'd met him. "I love you."

He paused, startled. Then his smile warmed even further. "I love you."

He bent to kiss her, stealing her breath away as he drank from her lips. When he lifted his head again, he gave her a wink. "I'm glad I said it first."

* * * * *

*To purchase and read more
books by Piper J. Drake, please visit her website at
http://piperjdrake.com.*

**Now available from Carina Press
and Piper J. Drake**

Meet the men of Centurion Corporation—an elite group
of mercenaries who will go to any extreme to complete
a mission…even risk their hearts. A new high-stakes
series by Piper J. Drake.

He's not the hero she's looking for.

As part of the elite Centurion Corporation team,
military-veteran-turned-mercenary Gabriel Diaz is a
natural defender. He'll do anything to ensure a mission
is successful. Anything but get emotionally invested—
he learned the hard way that can be deadly. Easy bodyguard jobs in between the more challenging missions
are all he's interested in now.

Maylin Cheng is desperate and running out of time.
Her younger sister has gone missing but no one seems
to take her concern seriously. Her last hope lies in asking an aloof bodyguard for help. He dismisses her outright, but all that changes when she is almost killed in
a not-so-accidental hit-and-run right before his eyes.

As Maylin leans on Gabriel, she begins to rely on
him for more than just her safety. But as their attraction
grows, so does the danger surrounding them. When the
elaborate web they're trapped in unravels, Gabriel will
do anything to protect them. Even if that means putting
his heart in the crosshairs.

Book one of the Safeguard series

Acknowledgments

Thank you to Philippa Ballantine for your advice regarding New Zealand culture and language. Also for late-night video fun with kakapos. Any mistakes in this story are completely mine.

Thank you to Angela James and Courtney Miller-Callihan for your understanding, encouragement and support.

About the Author

Piper J. Drake is an author of bestselling romantic suspense and edgy contemporary romance, a frequent flyer, and day job road warrior. She is often distracted by dogs, cupcakes, and random shenanigans.

Play Find the Piper online:
PiperJDrake.com
Facebook.com/AuthorPiperJDrake
Twitter @PiperJDrake
Instagram.com/PiperJDrake

Get 4 FREE REWARDS!

We'll send you 2 FREE Books
plus 2 FREE Mystery Gifts.

Harlequin® Romantic Suspense books feature heart-racing sensuality and the promise of a sweeping romance set against the backdrop of suspense.

FREE Value Over **$20**

YES! Please send me 2 FREE Harlequin® Romantic Suspense novels and my 2 FREE gifts (gifts are worth about $10 retail). After receiving them, if I don't wish to receive any more books, I can return the shipping statement marked "cancel." If I don't cancel, I will receive 4 brand-new novels every month and be billed just $4.99 per book in the U.S. or $5.74 per book in Canada. That's a savings of at least 12% off the cover price! It's quite a bargain! Shipping and handling is just 50¢ per book in the U.S. and 75¢ per book in Canada*. I understand that accepting the 2 free books and gifts places me under no obligation to buy anything. I can always return a shipment and cancel at any time. The free books and gifts are mine to keep no matter what I decide.

240/340 HDN GMYZ

Name (please print)

Address   Apt. #

City   State/Province   Zip/Postal Code

> Mail to the **Reader Service:**
> **IN U.S.A.:** P.O. Box 1341, Buffalo, NY 14240-8531
> **IN CANADA:** P.O. Box 603, Fort Erie, Ontario L2A 5X3

Want to try two free books from another series? Call 1-800-873-8635 or visit www.ReaderService.com.

---

*Terms and prices subject to change without notice. Prices do not include applicable taxes. Sales tax applicable in N.Y. Canadian residents will be charged applicable taxes. Offer not valid in Quebec. This offer is limited to one order per household. Books received may not be as shown. Not valid for current subscribers to Harlequin® Romantic Suspense books. All orders subject to approval. Credit or debit balances in a customer's account(s) may be offset by any other outstanding balance owed by or to the customer. Please allow 4 to 6 weeks for delivery. Offer available while quantities last.

Your Privacy—The Reader Service is committed to protecting your privacy. Our Privacy Policy is available online at www.ReaderService.com or upon request from the Reader Service. We make a portion of our mailing list available to reputable third parties that offer products we believe may interest you. If you prefer that we not exchange your name with third parties, or if you wish to clarify or modify your communication preferences, please visit us at www.ReaderService.com/consumerschoice or write to us at Reader Service Preference Service, P.O. Box 9062, Buffalo, NY 14240-9062. Include your complete name and address.

HRS18

Get 4 FREE REWARDS!

We'll send you 2 FREE Books plus 2 FREE Mystery Gifts.

Harlequin® Intrigue books feature heroes and heroines that confront and survive danger while finding themselves irresistibly drawn to one another.

FREE Value Over **$20**

Get 4 FREE REWARDS!

We'll send you 2 FREE Books plus 2 FREE Mystery Gifts.

FREE
Value Over
$20

Both the **Romance** and **Suspense** collections feature compelling novels written by many of today's best-selling authors.
